SIMON WARD

Time to Click

I would like to thank Steph and Phil for their proofreading and a huge thanks to the Shark Tank writing Group for their ongoing critique and support.

First edition

ISBN: 9798797982197

This book was professionally typeset on Reedsy.
Find out more at reedsy.com

Contents

Chapter 1

A cool rotten dampness woke Ethan from his daze, but his head felt like it was going to explode. Beads of sweat ran down his face, his throbbing head trapped inside a dark gauze bag. Every pulse of blood delivered more pain. His eyes wanted to welcome the light through the tiny holes, but he only experienced needles of torture from the morning light above him. He pulled at the hood to remove it, but a tight cord held it around his neck. As his senses returned, he ran his trembling fingers along the cord to find the knot. He tugged several times at the thin cord and the rough gauze hood, his frustration growing with each failed attempt. Hearing birds pecking close to him unnerved him further. He swung his arms towards them, and a flurry of flapping feathers appeared to leave the ditch. He slumped back against the dirt as pulses of pain forced him to rest.

Ten minutes must have passed before the pain eased enough for him to think more clearly. His hands touched the damp ground and he reached out to find a solid wall of dirt. He stood and reached up, but the wall of dirt continued past his reach. A stench permeated his gauze hood, the rotting whiff bringing a gag reflex and the knowledge something, or someone was in the ditch with him. He listened for something, only to hear his own breath, but he sensed something was close. He held his breath for a few seconds, yet still heard nothing.

"Help! Can somebody help me?" He called through the hood, but his muffled call went unanswered.

He crawled his way along the dirt wall to a corner and then another. The next corner would've given him some kind of clarity as he tried to gain his bearings, but when his hand reached out, it quickly retracted at the source of the stench. An unmistakable contact with someone's ribs felt through a thin shirt. Ethan frantically backed away until he hit a dirt wall. "Wake up! We need to get out of here!"

He didn't expect a response and didn't get one.

"Is anybody out there?" he whispered, not wanting further pain slicing through his head.

He waited, but the flapping of a couple of birds returning to the other end of the ditch was the only response.

He stepped forward a couple of paces and waved his arms. The birds flapped their wings and left them in silence.

"How did I end up in a ditch?" He had no recollection, but with the cold biting, he knew he needed to move. With a hood tied to his head, he was going nowhere. He tried again to release the knot, but the cold numbed his fingers.

He put his hands down his pants to warm them, but found smooth tape over his groin. Attempting to find the reassuring feel of his manhood, he found a thin tube protruding from the tape; it ran down his leg to a catheter bag. "What the fuck!" he screamed, and pain exploded again through his head. "What the hell has happened to me?" He murmured. He curled up into a ball with his arms crossed into his chest, hoping to gain some sense of touch to his numb fingers whilst he waited for the shooting pains in his head to ease.

Calmer, with his hands a little warmer and the pounding in

his head more manageable, he tried again to find the knot. His fingers ran along the cord to the back of his neck, and he found it. He tried to loosen the knot, containing the frustration of failure until the numbness returned to his fingers and he curled up again to warm his hands. Hoping for some understanding of his predicament to arrive, he lay still, but nothing came to him.

On the fifth attempt, he loosened the cord and through the tightest of gaps, he dragged the hood off his head. The bright sunlight directly above the ditch blinded his deprived eyes. The pain in his head struck deep again, and he covered his eyes with the very hood that had imprisoned them.

The warmth of the sun had barely registered before clouds took the edge off the stark light. The pain in his head calmed as the cold air swept away the heat in his head and his eyes adjusted. He could see the hood more clearly, and he tried to recall how he ended up in such a state. Nothing.

He glanced up from the hood to see two crows pecking away at the other guys' body. One was pecking out his eyes, whilst the other was pecking holes in his flesh. Ethan kicked out at them, causing a pull of discomfort in his groin, but after a flap into the air, they returned to their feed.

Ethan slowly rose to his feet, and the crows flapped away. Feeding time was over. The ditch was deep; he was not short, but he'd need to be a basketball pro to reach the edge of what appeared to be a double width grave plot.

After several vain attempts to jump and hold, he stared at the decaying, pecked body.

"Sorry, fella." Ethan muttered to the corpse before he tried to launch himself up, using the rotting body as a step. Ethan's foot, however, went straight through his chest, covering his calf in blood, guts, and maggots. "Great." Ethan looked down at his sorry state, lifting his foot out of the mess of rotten flesh and gagging once again at the stench as he brushed a few maggots off his leg.

Ethan stepped back from the body. "I will not die waiting for someone to rescue me." It hadn't helped the other guy. He needed to use all the resources he had available to him. A rotting corpse, a gauze hood and some cord.

A solution came to Ethan, but he'd have to hold back on throwing up. He stared at the deceased guy and bowed his head. "Lord. Thank you for the life of this guy and forgive me for the appalling yet necessary actions I need to take to avoid the same fate. Help me, Lord, to free myself of this wretched ditch. Amen."

Chapter 2

"Hi Mom," Ethan said, letting himself into his folks' place.

His Mom was in the kitchen preparing their meal. "Can you get your dad out of his workshop and to the table?"

"What you up to?" Ethan said, when he found him sitting at a bench with his magnifying glass, looking at a small processor.

"Vacuum is on the blink. Emptied its load in the hall again."

"Why don't you let me have a look?"

"I like to tinker."

Ethan patted his dad on his shoulder. "Tinkering's over for now. Dinner's ready."

After chatting about his job, his dad returned the subject to Ethan's non-existent love life. "When are you going to bring a young lady around to meet us?"

"Just need the time to build one." Ethan laughed but was met with sneers.

After dinner, his dad had a private word with Ethan. "You could do with finding a partner. I'm sure you'd rather be out to dinner with people of your own age rather than eating with me and your mom."

"It's not as easy as you'd think. I had a few online dates, but the world is full of crazy people. It was different at Uni. I had Mirek aside me and the women were smart. The last date

I went on, the crazy bitch wanted to ditch the restaurant and screw me before the starters had arrived. I hadn't even had chance to ask her anything."

"Was she any good?" his dad smiled.

Ethan returned a deadpan expression. "I made my excuses and left. I'm looking for somebody to click with."

"Why don't you change your search profile to show you want to settle down?"

"I did, and the loopy level just increased."

"Maybe you should just enjoy the sex. It might lead to something more meaningful."

"Or maybe not. The dating sites present either the nymphomaniac crazies who want rough sex or women who have nothing to say about anything other than make up and fitness."

"You could head into town with a mate from work for some old school dating?"

"The straight ones are all married or they're just kids."

"How about someone from the cricket team you used to play with?"

"Think most got married." Ethan's face lit up with the thought of a confirmed bachelor he used to know. "It's not a bad idea, I'll look up James, he's probably still single."

* * *

The following day, his conversation with his dad had been forgotten as he was in his favourite world, repairing robot vacuum cleaners and the occasional housebot at Baileys Electronics.

On top of his work, he headed back to his folks' place for a lunchtime snack. As usual, he let himself in, but his mom was not in the kitchen and his dad wasn't in his workshop. He heard his mom let out a loud moan and he darted towards the conservatory. Ethan would never erase the picture of what he saw before him. His dad's wrinkly bottom clenching as he drove into his mom, bent over the patio furniture and moaning her pleasure. Ethan quickly turned tail and left them to it. Seeing his parents having sex was something that would be hard to shift from his mind. He knew his parents had been getting more sex than him, given he wasn't getting any after turning his back on the dating sites, but seeing them at it was the shove he needed to get out more.

As he headed back to work, he gave himself a good talking to. "I'm in the prime of my life, reasonably good looking, and I'm in decent shape." He continued to berate himself, "If I don't do something, I'll end up alone."

After his internet dating troubles, he'd lost confidence and became more nervous around women. He certainly needed some help, but the guys who'd invited him to their nuptials were now happily under the thumb.

The writing had been on the wall. With each wedding, less of the old crew had been at the bar, until he'd become the last man standing. There remained one entry he'd overlooked, James Walker. They'd played in the college cricket team together before he left for Uni. His dominant memory of James was not of cricket, he was a different type of player. James could charm the birds from the trees. The last he heard from him, he was juggling three girls and was gloating about his breakfast, dinner and tea combo, after bedding them all in one day.

Desperate times, as they say. When he called James, he'd felt as nervous as he had with the internet dating failures, but fortunately James remembered him fondly from his cricketing

7

exploits and immediately suggested a catch-up drink.

They met up the next night. Ethan had planned a quiet pint at the local, but James convinced him to head into town. They moved onto a club to check out the local talent and had a few drinks, then a few more.

"Why don't you join our cricket team and re-awaken your college skills?" James asked.

"Don't know if I'm good enough." Ethan shrugged.

"You were excellent in college. A tricky spin bowler who claimed many a victory, I recall." James patted Ethan's back. "Come on. It'll be a blast, and the women love a cricketer."

James was right, but it hadn't got Ethan any female admirers. "I seem to remember it was you batting guys who had the women swooning."

James returned a knowing smile and crossed his legs to show off the inscription on the instep of his tanned leather boots, Another Six. "I guess seeing me smash a six gets them horny." He laughed and added, "Stick with me. You'll not go far wrong."

"Guess it's worth a go." Ethan thought he'd finished with his bowling days, but it would help to get him out more and being a wingman to James would be a good conversation opener.

"We've got a superb group of lads, but if I'm honest, we do more socializing than batting." James lifted his pint to chink their glasses. "Anyway, you won't find any fresh at the local unless Betty has some new teeth," James added.

"Think I'll give Betty a miss and join you at the crease, suppose it'll keep me fit."

James didn't seem to hear Ethan; he'd become distracted and had been staring past Ethan. Ethan raised his hand in front of James to regain his attention and he finally responded. "You might even find some tasty bird to click with. Just like that angel over there." James pointed out a little lady he'd had his eye on. Her friend, who looked like she'd be more comfortable on a rugby field, got up to get another drink and left her friend alone with a dainty glass of white wine. "Sorry Mate, if I'm taking her home tonight, I'd better introduce myself whilst her bodyguard is away."

Ethan watched on and sure enough, James and the little lady made a swift connection. When her large friend returned, James immediately pointed in Ethan's direction. Ethan darted away to evade her attention. The hasty move reminded him he was not used to the club scene or the heavy drinking. His head spun. He leant against a pillar to regain his balance whilst keeping out of view. His focus returned when a friendly brunette gave him a smile as she approached.

"Are you hiding?" she politely asked.

He smiled back, "not really," before he put out a hand to introduce himself.

She shook his hand like she was meeting a client. "Pleased to meet you."

"I'm Ethan. I've not drank much since my Uni days. I'm struggling."

She giggled. "Me too," she'd probably intended to whisper in his ear but bellowed out, "I'm also hiding, from an overbearing gorilla. Shall we go upstairs? It's comfier and much quieter." She led Ethan to the chill out lounge and pointed him to the bar for two bottles of water before she dropped onto some cozy seats in a small booth. Initially, Ethan thought she was using him as a shield, but she seemed genuinely interested when he talked about his job and she didn't appear crazy. Her lips hadn't been pumped up and she wasn't plastered with make-

9

up. When Ethan pointed to the back of his wrist to show her where the crypto payment chip had been inserted. It did not as impress her as he thought it would, but when she stroked the back of her own wrist, she declared, "got mine three weeks ago."

"I heard they tickle if you don't use them often enough."

"Mine's been fine so far, but I use it every day." Rachel smiled and placed her mobile over the back of Ethan's hand. "Didn't you include your ID?"

"Nope, just the payment chip."

They'd definitely hit it off and now had something in common. She seemed to gain more interest in him as he talked about the closeness he had with his parents. "Stable families make stable people," she said. "You're lucky. My parents split up a few months ago."

"It must be difficult," Ethan said, nodding appropriately.

She waved away his offer of sympathy. "I've remained fairly stable so far. Not gone sex mad, like my mom." She laughed it off and playfully pushed Ethan. "But that could all change."

Was she joking? Ethan tested the water and placed his hand on her knee, but got a smack on his hand to confirm she'd indeed been joking. It was the first genuine connection Ethan had experienced with a girl for a long time. He'd had a few brief relationships at college, but this girl felt like a good fit. They were so comfortable chatting together. Was this the girl to click with, or were they relaxed because they were both drunk? They fell asleep together in their booth, but a security droid woke them and suggested it was time for them to go home. "Shall we go back to my place?" Ethan suggested as they headed for the exit.

"No, thanks. I like to sleep in my own bed," her abrupt

response.

Ethan could sense another failure as conversation halted and she tapped her mobile to message a taxi. "I'd like to see you again," Ethan blurted out. He paused for a moment as she took in his words and turned back to him. "What's your name?" he asked.

She laughed at the situation before she explained. "Ethan, you've been chatting with me for a few hours." She smirked. "And we've already kinda slept together." She folded her arms. "You've asked me to your place, but not asked my name."

Ethan had no response.

"I'm Rachel. Shall I give you my number." She rolled her eyes. He was obviously no player. She produced an eyeliner stick from her slim clutch bag and pulled up his sleeve to write her number on his arm. "I can't believe you don't have a device with you. Perhaps you should add your ID to the chip in your wrist."

"It's not a bad idea. I kept losing mobiles on drunken nights out when I was at college, didn't keep a phone long enough to remember the number. I have a coms watch, but the strap's bust.

"If only you knew an engineer." Rachel shook her head, but her mouth curled up into another smile. "If you want to see me again, put it in your device when you get home, before you shower it off in the morning," she instructed him.

"Good Idea, Rachel. That's right, Rachel?"

"I've written it on your arm," her taxi arrived, and the door opened.

"No worries, I'll call you tomorrow," he said, pulling his sleeve back down.

She ran back to him, gave him a peck on his cheek and dived

11

into her taxi. The taxi door closed, and it smoothly pulled away, to leave Ethan holding onto the memory of her lips on his cheek and her delicate vanilla scent.

Ethan didn't need a taxi; he floated most of the way home in a dreamy haze until the alcohol and tiredness hit. He staggered on until he got to the welcome sight of his front door; After a couple of failed attempts, he opened his door, dragged himself up the stairs and dropped onto his bed to dream about how things may move on with Rachel.

Chapter 3

The following morning, Ethan awoke groggy and headed for the shower to kick start his day. He stood under the hot revitalizing drench and pressed his forehead against the glass. His head was pounding from his excesses as he tried to piece together the previous night.

He'd met someone. He remembered her perfect smile, the calming vanilla scent, the comfy chat and the quick kiss before she disappeared in a taxi. Ethan recalled her last words to him were 'write it down.' He stared at his arm to see the evidence before him, but he'd smudged the name and number. Without grabbing a towel, Ethan stepped out of the shower to note down the details. He could read Rachel, but a couple of digits from her number were unclear.

"I'll just call all the possible numbers." He pondered for a moment before returning to the warmth of the shower. The shower got his brain working and gave him an idea. "I'll send multiple texts instead, much easier than ringing strangers."

Exiting the shower again, he grabbed a towel and sat on the sofa to tap in all the number variations. "Would like to see you tonight if that's ok, Ethan." Sent. Ethan re-entered the shower, proud of his great idea. "I think she had brown hair."

After his shower, he lay on the bed thinking about the

previous night, which then became a dream as he drifted off. His phone awoke him. His college buddy James had rung to check he'd got back safely. "Sorry about leaving you to fend off the women. I got transfixed by a rare beauty." James continued to explain how she'd been more interesting than his usual prey.

"No worries. I found my own piece of treasure last night, Rachel. Not sure if I'll see her again, though." Ethan explained about losing the number.

James cut off Ethan's explanation. "Are you coming for the get together at the cricket club?"

Ethan agreed to go along. "It'll be better than spending the afternoon staring at my phone."

As Ethan was contemplating popping to his mom's for breakfast, his phone beeped with a text and it read, "I thought I wouldn't hear from you. I'm in the village doing some shopping." Success at last, he texts straight back, "I live above the butchers in Rose Village. Come on up, bring some bacon for breakfast."

"On my way," she replied.

The knock on the door had his pulse racing as he rushed to open it, but when he opened the door, he had to force a smile, as he didn't recognize her. He'd been drunk but was totally perplexed as she waltzed in with a bright, "morning." She grabbed a frying pan, and the aroma of sizzling bacon soon filled the room. He tried to tidy up a little as she prepared a bacon sandwich. "Butty time," she called.

"Nothing like a bacon butty, after a heavy night's drinking."

"Guess not," she said as she sat down next to him on the two-seater sofa. They dived into their respective butties; Ethan returned a cute grin when she smiled through a mouthful of sandwich. Ethan didn't know what to say. His shyness had returned without the drink to loosen his tongue. She appeared happy to just be sitting with him. When she finished her sandwich, she asked if she could use the bathroom. She stopped on the way and seductively turned back and bit her lip.

Ethan had a momentary flashback and recalled that last night she had light brown hair, yet the girl in his bathroom was blond. Was he still confused? Had she worn a wig or was this someone else?

When she re-appeared, she'd applied some red lipstick and was wearing a playful smile.

"Do you want to dance with me?" She asked. She tilted her head and swept her hair behind her ear.

Ethan was not comfortable with the way she was offering herself to him. Before he had chance to answer, she reached out with both hands to pull him up. As he rose, she guided his hands under her short skirt to her bare butt; she grabbed his hair and launched a mighty suck onto his lips before driving her tongue into his mouth. Finally, she released him to breathe and tried to pull down his joggers.

He held on to them and quizzed her. "What's got into you? You weren't like this last night."

"What do you mean last night?" her puzzled reply, as she tried to put her hand down his pants.

Ethan finally realized what was happening. He pushed her away. "Who are you?"

She held her hands out. "What's the problem? You called me up here."

"You're not Rachel, the girl I met last night."

"How pissed were you?" she sarcastically replied.

"Not used to the drink. Why did you come up here?"

"I thought you were a guy I'd seen before, who wanted to

fuck."

"You don't even know me!" he exclaimed.

She shrugged. "I know, but I thought you were cute. Why not jump you anyway?"

"Sorry to disappoint. I like to know the people I have sex with." He sounded like a prudish church girl.

"Well, you know me now." She asked hopefully with a finger and thumb stroking her chin.

He rolled his eyes and shook his head. "You need help."

"Will you give it to me?" she tilted her head and gave him a cute girly smile.

"That would be a no! Please leave."

"Can't leave yet. Someone needs to finish me off."

Ethan picked up the bag of meat by the door and thrust it towards her. "That's the only meat you're getting. Now piss off."

She snatched the bag of meat, slapped his face and stormed off.

Ethan's hands were shaking. He'd never been comfortable with confrontation and as much as most women were forward, that crazy was off the scale. He found solace in a cup of tea and switched on the radio. Love songs played and his mind returned to Rachel.

"She definitely had brown hair."

* * *

His phone rang, but the tingle of excitement for Rachel was dashed when it was his mom. All the same, he accepted the invitation to lunch and a game of dominoes, rather than any delights an afternoon with Rachel may have brought. He changed out of his joggers and put on a shirt and tie to please his mom. She always liked him smartly dressed.

With the wrist device strap still broken, he picked up his mobile and headed for the door. "Mobiles and drinking don't mix." Knowing he was meeting up with James later, he placed the mobile back in the flat and dived out the door.

Over lunch, his parents were pleased to hear he was getting out and couldn't play dominoes all afternoon. They wished him well as he set off for the cricket club. Ethan was nervous about meeting the cricket guys but soon settled down with a pint or two. James had been spot on. They did more socializing than playing; they'd only met to have a few pints to welcome Ethan to the team. Ethan's sporting prowess had preceded him, and they were happy to get him on board. Several pints in, Ethan was ready to head home and check his phone.

He had a relaxing stroll back to the flat, feeling more confident his social life had sprung into action. As soon as he got into his flat, he checked his phone. He had eight replies, six with wrong number references, but two who could have been Rachel. The first read, "it's knitting tonight, call me at 9pm." Was this some old lady who was up for a fling? The second was more promising. "Come to 24 Heron Close tonight at 8pm."

He ignored the first one and replied to the second, "OK, see you later."

After nodding off in front of the TV, he awoke with Rachel on his mind. He thought about her as he freshened up. Second time lucky, with a spring in his step, he headed towards Heron Close. His mind was clear as he remembered her face and the smile she'd given him as she dived into the cab. He bounced along, eager to taste her kiss again.

His confidence ebbed away as he neared the door. He contemplated for a moment how this could be another weirdo, but it was worth the risk to see Rachel again. He tentatively tapped on the door and waited with both fear and excitement. A middle-aged, slender man opened the door.

"Is this the r-right house? I'm looking for R-Rachel." He had never stammered before and his cheeks burst into flames with embarrassment.

"Yes, mate," came the friendly reply to calm Ethan's nerves. "She's not ready. You'd better come in and wait."

"No problem." He tried to maintain his fragile confidence and appear cool as he entered the living room. Ethan took a seat and settled down to watch some TV, feeling relieved to have found his Rachel.

"I'll tell her you're here," his host said calmly, before heading upstairs.

A few moments later, he came halfway down the stairs. "She'll be down in a minute. She said you should put this on." He threw Ethan a blindfold.

"What's this for?" Ethan asked.

"I don't know what she's up to. Just roll with it. Anyway, nice to meet you. I've got an early shift. I'm off to bed. Have an enjoyable night."

"Cheers Mate, Night."

The man called again to Rachel, "Don't keep the lad waiting."

Ethan declined to put on the eye mask, opting to watch the TV.

Five minutes later, he heard her gentle voice. "Put the mask on."

He wanted to turn to see her again, but opted for the fun and slipped the mask over his eyes.

She tapped her nails on the banister as she descends the stairs, giving Ethan goosebumps of excitement. He heard her approaching and smiled. "This is not the kinda date I was expecting, but I'm open to new experiences."

She didn't respond, but he could hear her containing a snigger as she drew closer. He jumped as she tapped the couch from behind him. Her lacey glove stroked his cheek, and she slid her finger gently down his chest to his stomach. Ethan relaxed as she traced a delicate finger around his already bulging trousers.

"Is it my turn?" Ethan asked as he raised his hand.

She firmly slapped his hand with no further response, and Ethan returned his stinging hand to his side.

She unbuttoned his trousers and pulled at the band of his shorts. When the lace covered hand touched his dick, Ethan objected. "Woah! You're more forward than you were at the club. Don't I get a kiss first?"

She came in close and delivered a less than delicate kiss to his lips.

It wasn't a good kiss. He lifted the mask and holding his dick was the guy who'd welcomed him in, with the addition of bright red lipstick and a summer dress. Ethan pushed him to the floor and dived for the door as the guy tried to grab his leg.

"Don't go, it was just getting interesting," he complained as Ethan shot out of the door.

Once outside, Ethan nearly knocked over an old couple taking their dog a walk as mid sprint he tucked his tackle back into his pants.

"Bloody pervert," the old man shouted. Ethan had no desire to complain or explain and carried on running. Having had enough excitement for the evening, he headed back home for the more familiar world of internet TV as he despatched a flurry of beers, hoping to clear the image from his brain.

Chapter 4

The sun had not quite reached Ethan's room, but the buzz of a text message stirred him. He stretched over and grabbed his phone for the next instalment in his newly active social life. "Did the knitting put you off?" The message read.

Not ready for a repeat of the previous nights, cross dressing action, he decided it would be better to call.

"Hello." The light yet positive voice answered.

"Is that Rachel?" he tentatively asked.

"Were you drunk again last night?" A smile spread across his face as he recognised her voice.

He thought quickly. "Had an early night."

"Did the knitting comment put you off? I take my grandma."

"Thought I had the wrong number when you mentioned knitting."

"Did you wash it off in the shower, then?" He could tell she was smiling.

"Nearly. Saw it just in time."

"Would you like to go for a walk later?"

Ethan wished he could ask a girl on a date with such comfort. "Would love to. Where shall we go?"

"Shall we meet at St. Stevens Park? How about one o'clock by the fountain?"

Ethan agreed, and after ending the call, he danced around his flat in his boxers. "Looks like today will be better than yesterday." After two strange, sort of liaisons, he couldn't wait to see Rachel again.

He wanted to look chilled out, so he went for the jeans and trainers with a tee shirt and a light hooded jacket. When he arrived, his apprehension rose, half expecting another mad date as he walked through the park. The moment he got sight of the fountain, he spotted Rachel leaning against it with her face capturing the warming summer rays. She looked fantastic wearing tight black jeans and a yellow and grey striped top.

A calm descended over him, and the cool, confident Ethan appeared. She turned and smiled when she heard his footsteps approach. "Hiya."

"Hi." He returned a smile and held out his hand to shake.

Following his formal lead, she shook his hand like she was meeting a business client. "Glad you could make it." She pointed to the path, "shall we begin our walk."

He laughed at her mirrored response to his formal handshake. "Yes, let's. Rachel isn't it," he continued with the exchange, much to Rachel's amusement. As they walked along, Ethan relaxed, and the conversation flowed naturally as it had done at the club.

They were both enjoying a peaceful walk together until they heard a muffled scream. They quickened their pace towards the scream and noticed a beefy guy with a bald head pinning a woman's neck to the tree with a vice-like grip. Ethan recognized the girl. It was the visitor to his flat who'd made him a sandwich and tried to have sex with him.

"Steady on fella. You're hurting the poor girl." Ethan said bravely to the guy towering over his prey.

"Walk away!" he replied to Ethan, before turning his attention back to the girl. "Who were you with last night?" He bellowed for the entire park to hear.

"Nobody," she pleaded, and glanced in Ethan's direction.

Don't look at me, Ethan thought. The guy threw her to the ground and his focus returned to Ethan.

"Was it you?" he growled.

"He was with me," Rachel said as she grabbed Ethan's arm and pulled him away. As soon as they were out of earshot, she glared at Ethan. "You seemed to recognize her. Were you with her last night?"

He raised his hands in defence and shook his head. "No. She looks like someone I met once, but I've not been with her. Last night, I was alone with some beers watching the game on TV." Ethan didn't figure that telling Rachel about his early morning caller would paint him in a good light, even though he'd nothing to hide. If he had, he'd have been in more danger from Rachel from the frown on her face.

The woman screamed out again, and they looked back to see him push her down behind a bush and he appeared to be kicking her.

Ethan looked up to the sky to see an observation drone approaching. "The drone will alert the police; it's best we keep out of it."

"He's going to kill her," Rachel said, her feet planted in fear for the woman.

"He'll kill us too if we get in the way." Ethan grabbed Rachel by the hand and turned her away. "The police will be here soon."

Rachel tapped at her phone.

"What are you doing?" Ethan nervously glanced back,

hoping the guy didn't see Rachel making a call.

"Emergency. Violent assault in St. Stevens Park. Woman injured. Needs urgent help." Rachel quickly said before she ended the call as promptly as she'd made it. She slipped her phone into her pocket. "I feel better now."

Ethan shook his head and took Rachel by the hand to resume their pacey exit from the situation. They slowed as they entered a narrow pergola tunnel dense with Ivy. It was idyllic and could have been a romantic moment if not for the heavy steps slapping the tarmac closer and closer behind them. Rachel squeezed Ethan's hand and glanced at him for assurance. Ethan glanced back, hoping it was a jogger, but the beefy attacker was following them into the pergola tunnel to evade the drone hovering above.

Rachel had her back to him and was blocking his route. Ethan pulled Rachel towards him, and she let out a scream as the guy sped past them. Rachel looked into Ethan's eyes and put her arms around him. Ethan held her tight in his embrace, attempting to contain both of their adrenaline fuelled trembles. "He'd have knocked you clean over." She rested her head on his neck and Ethan gave her a delicate kiss on the side of her temple. As he took in a proud breath through his nostrils, he took in her sweet vanilla scent and Rachel held him tighter. Finally, he had someone to hold and protect.

"Shall we check on the girl?" Ethan said and led Rachel back towards her. A crowd had gathered, and a security drone was hovering by where she lay, which prompted Ethan to stop. "Let's not be part of the staring crowd."

"There's a nice little coffee shop on the other side of the park." Rachel pointed. "I need coffee."

"Yeah, I need coffee too." Ethan took Rachel by the hand,

and they attempted to put the chilling episode behind them. As Ethan paced towards the coffee shop, the previously dominant Rachel scampered along with him.

A drone was hovering above the park café as they approached, but Rachel was eager for her coffee fix. Her eagerness soon disappeared when they entered and she saw the attacker in the same grey hoodie, stretching his wide jaw around a sandwich. She tugged at Ethan before he could order and all but dragged him out of the coffee shop. Ethan looked at her as if she'd gone mad. "I thought you wanted coffee."

"Didn't you see him in there?" Ethan glanced back into the café, but Rachel pulled him away. "Walk me home."

The sound of sirens entering the park made passing out through the wrought-iron gates a relief, but Ethan couldn't get the thought out of his head. The guy had probably killed the woman. He should've done more. He'd have been no match for the huge muscle-bound guy, but he may have stopped her from getting murdered. Thankfully, Rachel hadn't urged him to get involved. Perhaps seeing her new boyfriend get pummelled was not her idea of a perfect date.

Oblivious to Ethan's remorse, Rachel's grasp on his arm calmed as she talked passionately about her job as an estate agent. "I've sold nearly a hundred houses to help people onto the property market, but I haven't bought one for myself yet."

"Why, haven't you got a rental on the go?"

"Saving for my own, so I can leave home and be rid of my mom and Brad." She strained at saying Brad's name.

Ethan left the subject of Brad and focussed on his place. "Got mine years ago. I used to rent it out. When the last guy moved out, I figured it was time for me to leave home. I still pop to my mom's for her cooking, though."

Rachel smiled, likely happy that he hadn't dwelled on Brad. "Don't tell me she does your washing too," she asked, returning some fun to the chat.

"I love my place. You should come over and check it out?" Ethan didn't admit his mom still sorted his laundry.

"Think I've had enough excitement for today. I want to go home."

They reached Rachel's tidy looking family home. It was like his parents' place, but he was most impressed with the cool wheels on the drive.

"Is that your mom's?" Ethan said, looking at a grey convertible Porsche. It was grey, but the showroom guys would have said diamond silver.

"Brad's." Rachel snapped back and screwed up her face.

Ethan responded with hands aloft and his brow raised, "O.K." as he stepped back.

Rachel's mood changed right back as she giggled at Ethan's comical response.

Ethan hoped he may get an invitation in for coffee, either the hot drink variety or the hot and steamy preferred option, but Rachel stood with the door behind her protecting what lay inside.

"Maybe the park's not such a good place. Would you like to come around to mine next time for a movie?" Ethan asked.

"I'd prefer a meal out, followed by a movie in the town?" Rachel replied as she gave him a cheeky smile.

"Only if it's comedy. I've had enough horror." Ethan was pleased he'd talked so freely. Things were looking up. He was finally clicking with someone.

They agreed and set the date for the following evening.

"See you tomorrow." Ethan turned to go, but Rachel rushed

back to him and gave him a peck on the cheek before she disappeared inside her house giving the door a firm click shut.

Rachel running back to him for a kiss, put him on cloud nine. She liked him for sure, but she'd declined the offer of going back to his place again.

As Ethan walked home, the events in the park caught up with him. He pictured the girl's battered face looking up at him. He wondered if the girl would not have been abused, if he'd entertained her after she made him a butty, but then again, maybe that was the reason she'd ended up in a sorry state.

When he got back to his flat, he found a voicemail on his mobile from James Walker, who'd rang him to gloat over his latest conquest of Kate the angel, from their night out and how he thought she could be the one for him. Ethan called him back and told him about his traumatic walk in the park and how he'd got a follow-up date for the following night. James assured Ethan that he should take her back to his flat and do the deed, rather than wasting time going for a meal and a movie.

Ethan reflected on the call and thought perhaps advice from Casanova was not his best route to a long-term partner, but he'd jotted down a few impressive lines to use later to entice her back to the flat.

Chapter 5

Rachel had been in several brief relationships with some handsome and charming guys. Unfortunately, each either lost interest after they'd got her into bed, or she'd ditched them after catching them with lipstick on their collars. She got plenty of attention. Her healthy figure was an attractive alternative to the more fashionable stick-like barbie types parading the clubs, but avoiding the creeps was a challenge, especially when they were strong, good-looking guys.

As she was getting ready, she reflected on how Ethan was a reasonable-looking lad and a safer bet than the hunters she'd previously fell prey to, but Rachel knew also that despite his positive actions in the park, as yet he hadn't taken her in his arms and given her a proper kiss. She thought the kiss would happen after he'd walked her home, but the sight of Brad's car and him snooping out the window turned her off the idea.

She hoped their first kiss would be worth the wait and give her the warming glow she wanted. "Is he nervous about kissing me? Did I come over too assertive for him?" she asked herself as she gave the mirror a confident, unyielding look. She insisted to herself that she wouldn't go all limp and girly. If he was nervous about progressing things, he needed to man up. After a few failed relationships, her doubts re-surfaced. "Why didn't he kiss me? Does he fancy me or is he just after a quick fuck like the others?" On the basis he seemed like he wasn't a player, Rachel thought she'd probably need to encourage him. Having not had any for months, she wanted sex and if she needed to take charge, then so be it.

She told her mom she'd met a new guy and Brad chipped in his unwanted advice. "Don't shag him until you know you can trust him."

Rachel's cheeks burned with embarrassment, and she rushed back to her room. Whilst her cheeks cooled, she picked up the picture taken with her dad. Her mom had taken it when she graduated college. She could hardly wait till the weekend to tell him about Ethan.

She picked out four outfits and hung them on the outside of her wardrobe before heading into the shower. Whilst in the shower, she reflected on Brad's advice and thought that maybe she had sometimes been too trusting. In her previous relationships, she'd enjoyed the sex, but the disappointment that often followed dug deep and she needed a change of tactics. When she emerged from the shower, she returned all four outfits to the wardrobe and started again.

Eventually, she settled for long navy trousers and a flowery fitted blue and white blouse, then decided it looked too much like she was going to work and changed into her favourite fitted brown dress with printed red roses. She appeared after negotiating the stairs in her high heels to give her mom a twirl.

"Overdressed for the pictures, aren't you?" her mom said.

Rachel let out a frustrated groan and wiggled back upstairs. Five minutes later, she appeared again, this time in tight jeans, with a white blouse. Her stare towards her mom received a comment of, "much better."

Brad chipped in, "that's the idea. He won't get them off."

Rachel held back from telling him to fuck off and smiled sarcastically, before she said a quick goodbye to her mom and headed out to the awaiting taxi.

* * *

Showered and dressed a full two hours before he needed to meet Rachel. Ethan tidied up the flat, just in case she came back at the end of their date. After turning it into a show home, he thought it looked too tidy for a bachelor pad and threw a few clothes around to mess it up again.

He was wearing a shirt, with a tie which he kept loosening, then tightening again whilst he waited outside the restaurant. When Rachel rose out of the taxi, she looked the picture of cool. He strolled forward to meet her and paused before he said, "you look amazing." He'd said it confidently, but he had been practicing it for an hour. It was a routine line given to him by James, and it seemed to work. Rachel was beaming as Ethan took her hand and led her in through the busy bar area to the rear of the venue. Secluded dining booths provided a private area of tranquillity away from the heaving masses.

Ethan's nerves melted away and they talked about their eventful walk in the park. Rachel revealed, "I went weak at the knees when you pulled me towards you."

"The guy was about to knock you clean over. Glad you didn't mind," Ethan said.

Rachel held his hand over the table. "You were my hero, can't think of a better guy to have saved me."

Ethan tried to hide the heat in his cheeks. "Thank you,

madam. It was my pleasure." Ethan bowed his head like she was nobility.

They both chose the lamb shank and shared a bottle of red wine. Rachel chatted about how she'd sold another house and she asked Ethan about his work. He told her about how he'd re-wired one of the Tushi house bots. "Apparently, the lady of the house had gone psycho, and their daughter saved the bot from her mom, rather than the other way round." Ethan rubbed his hands together. "It pleased the boss. We didn't have to send it onto Tushi and said he'd got a special reward for me."

"Special reward? What's that a bonus?"

"I'm hoping for advanced training in America, but a bonus would also be good."

"More training doesn't sound like a bonus."

"It's the only way to progress to get the big bucks. I don't want to be stuck repairing machines my entire career."

"Ah. I get it. Delayed gratification. Not common now with instant everything."

"Some things are worth waiting for," Ethan replied with confidence.

"Indeed," Rachel replied with a broad smile before she dragged her teeth over her bottom lip. The realisation of the connection to sex brought a heat to Ethan's cheeks. He needed to change the subject.

"Do you like cricket?"

"Not really a big sports fan, full of jocks who think they're God's gift."

"I play cricket, don't think I qualify as a cocky jock though."

"I wouldn't be here if you were. It was rugby guys I was hiding from at the club. They wanted to pick me up. Literally."

Ethan laughed. "Cricket is more gentlemanly."

"Still not for me. I prefer music. I play piano."

Ethan nodded his approval. "Impressive. Where do you play?"

"Just at home. I'll play for you. If you promise not to invite me to the cricket."

Confident they'd clicked, Ethan tried another one of James's lines. "Shall we forget the movie and go back to mine?"

Rachel took exception to his suggestion and leant back in her chair. "We're going to the film; I've been looking forward to it."

Ethan mentally threw away James's chat lines and rued the comment. They finished the bottle of wine without speaking. Rachel seemed to enjoy the silence as she left Ethan with his thoughts.

The server dropped the bill on the table between them, and Ethan tried to lighten the mood. "Did I mention I was Dutch?" he smiled.

Rachel replied instantly, "did I mention I was from Greece. We don't pay for anything."

Whilst Rachel visited the ladies, Ethan settled the bill using the crypto chip in the back of his wrist, much to the surprise of the young server who thought he was a magician. Ethan loved the technology, but it wouldn't be long before everyone caught up with implanted tech.

Ethan's chance of catching the previews diminished as he watched the minutes pass on the clock projected above the bar. Rachel re-emerged after re-applying some lipstick. The warm smile she gave him made the waiting worth it. He held the door open for her and she stepped through like she was entering a film set. The cinema was only a short walk away and Ethan caught up to open the next door. Rachel paraded through with a polite nod. "Thank you, kind Sir."

Rachel insisted she pay for the tickets, whilst Ethan bought the drinks and popcorn. The previews were well in flow as they took their seats. Rachel confessed she'd not been to a cinema for ages and recounted a story of her first visit with a boy who'd tried fumbling on the back row, only to get a slap. Ethan didn't share his experience with the girl from work who'd stood him up, then laughed at him when he got to work the next day.

When the movie started, the opening scene had a girl strolling through a park. Rachel and Ethan glanced at each other. The girl in the movie jumped when a guy dashed past her. Rachel grabbed Ethan's hand and her wide eyes reminded him of her hero comment from earlier. Ethan's chest puffed out with pride. She wanted him; he was her hero.

Ethan slipped his hand over hers for a while until the temptation was too great and he slipped his hand back into the popcorn. Rachel's hand remained comfortable on his leg, something he wasn't used to. Should he return his hand to hers, place his hand on her leg, or carry on eating the popcorn. The popcorn won.

Ethan eventually settled down and relaxed into the film. He didn't want to fall asleep, which he often did watching films at home. The soda provided the sugar boost to keep him awake and avoided any embarrassing snores or dribbles down his chin.

As the closing credits appeared, they were comfortable together in their own little bubble, until another couple needed to get past. Ethan followed their lead, and they also left hand in hand. As they exited the cinema, a taxi was available, and they stepped right in. It was rare to see a driver seated up front.

The autonomous fleets had the lion's share of the business.

Annoyingly, the taxi driver rifled through question after question. Maybe the autonomous option would have been better. The driver said they looked good together and asked about their night before telling them about his family. They looked at each other and shared a visual joke as he talked about how his daughter had just met a nice bloke called James Walker and how he hoped she'd keep this one longer. Ethan kept it to himself how unlikely that would be.

As they arrived at Rachel's, the Porsche was missing. Ethan stepped out of the taxi, put his hand out for Rachel and walked her to her door. She fumbled with her keys, "It's been a great night, do you want to..."

Ethan's face lit up. "Come in for coffee."

"Second thoughts, better not. Work in the morning." Something had obviously spooked Rachel.

"Maybe next time," Ethan said. He stepped closer to kiss her, but she rested her head on his shoulder to share a warming embrace.

Ethan had a stirring in his loins. It was more than sexual arousal; it went deeper. But alas, all too soon, it was over. She gave him a gentle kiss on his cheek. Ethan's hand had been moving up her back to pull her in closer and share a passionate kiss, but she broke off their connection and turned back to open her door. In a flicker of a moment, she blew him a kiss and shut the door, leaving his hopes of being invited in strewn over the floor.

Despite not getting the coffee he'd hoped for, Ethan bounced along back to his flat. She'd certainly flicked a switch on for him. He'd never felt so alive. Ethan shared his beaming smile with several dog walkers as he passed them on the way back to his flat, each look mistaking love for intoxication.

When he arrived at the flat door, he burst through and leapt up the stairs with his newfound energy. He picked up his mobile to send a message of gratitude for his jolly state and an enjoyable night, only to find he already had a message. "Had a lovely night. Text back when you're home safe." He wished she'd delivered the following kissing emoji personally.

"I'm back. C U soon." Ethan followed it with a cool emoji after changing his mind about the kiss and a heart.

He lay in bed with his hands behind his head. Life was on the up.

* * *

Rachel was beaming too and proud of herself for not asking him in. She wanted to make love to him, but after a momentary wobble at the front door, she'd stuck to her plan. When she got the text back, she stopped staring out of the window and made her way upstairs and enjoyed her own smiling reflection in her mirror. "Take it slow, make it last." She lay on her bed with her hands behind her head and congratulated herself for her improved self-control.

Chapter 6

Heading into town for their next date, Ethan suggested, "How about trying the Groove." It was an 80s nightclub, which Ethan had yet to visit.

"No thanks, it's a dodgy place full of weirdos. Trust me, never go there," Rachel said, like an old man from a horror film warning the kids not to stay in the creepy old boathouse. "The Red Lion's better. It's the place to be seen." The extended popular pub was a huge venue with a full spectrum of evening entertainment from chill out lounges and dance rooms to a full complement of AR experiences.

It was a relaxing date for both Ethan and Rachel. They'd both been there before, but tonight they were there as a couple. With work the following day, they'd not planned on meeting any of their other buddies. They settled down in the quiet lounge, just chatting about their day. Rachel had sold a sizable property out of town, with a hefty commission cheque to follow. "I think meeting you gave me a boost. I'm on a roll lately."

Overawed by her increased sense of belief, Ethan just smiled and wondered where the anxious girl he met at the club had gone. She obviously still fancied him, and he fired back with equal confidence. "I must be your lucky charm."

"I guess you are." She said, chinking her wine glass against his.

It was an unfamiliar experience for Ethan to relax with a woman as confident as Rachel. All his previous short-lived relationships had been with shy girls who'd lacked confidence, and he hadn't changed their state, hence the lack of progress. Rachel was a smart girl, full of confidence. He was just trying to keep up.

When last orders called, Rachel checked her watch. "Can't believe where the time has gone."

"Was just thinking the same." He sat forward and casually asked, "would you like to come back to mine tonight?"

"I'd love to, but I've got an early viewing tomorrow. We don't want to be rushing things." Her lips curled into a smile, and she dragged her teeth over her bottom lip.

Ethan took in a deep breath through his nostrils. He wanted to make love to her on the very seat where she sat. Ethan wanted to reply that he wouldn't need long, but decided it may not give her the right impression of him. "The anticipation builds," he said as he stroked his chin.

Rachel replied with a quick shrug. "Sometimes that's the best part."

Ethan was holding back his sexual energy, like a lion eager to pounce. As they got up to leave, Ethan took her in his arms and their lips met. The intensity of their kiss deepened, and her arms wrapped around him. Ethan traced his hand down to the small of her back. He wanted to hold her ass in his hands, but it wasn't the place. When she politely broke off their kiss, Ethan put his hand out for her to lead the way. As she stepped in front of him, he addressed the discomfort in his groin whilst he admired her cute rear.

* * *

The fire in Rachel's core was blazing. She wanted to take him home, but work commitments helped her to keep control and stick to her guns. They left together, with Ethan clutching her waist as they dived into a taxi. Thankfully, no driver was there to interrupt the end of their evening, as they smooched all the way to Rachel's.

The tingles between her legs intensified and when the taxi beeped its arrival, the ride was over too soon. They shared another deep kiss before she slipped out of the taxi.

* * *

Back in his flat, he checked for a message from Rachel. "Let me know you're back safe. Btw, great kisser." Three kissing emojis followed it. "Not so bad yourself. Back safe," he replied and mirrored the emojis. He rested his mobile aside him and leant back to take in the whirlwind of Rachel that had him intoxicated with love. He was about to gratify himself when he got another text. The message was from James Walker. "Did you bang her then?"

Ethan shook his head at the directness of James's interest and replied with a discreet, "Talk tomorrow."

Ethan hoped that would be it, but his phone rang with a video call. James's face was one of fun. "Still not sealed the deal."

Ethan ignored his crude appraisal. "I'm pleased with the way it's going."

"Happy to be in the friend zone then," James said, before he added, "Did I waste my training on you?"

"Training? Any more of your suggested chat and I'll get slapped in the face again," Ethan said.

"Worked on the angel, Kate. She was mad for it, once I got her back to mine." James told Ethan in great detail, how he'd worked his magic on her. "Nailed the new barmaid at the cricket club this afternoon. Great rack."

Ethan shook his head. "Do you even care for these women?"

"Care for 'em? Absolutely. I love 'em all."

Ethan saw James's childish grin and shook his head disapprovingly. Not that it would have any effect on the serial Casanova. "You treat every woman like another six."

James lifted his boot to the phone. "Don't knock the sixes." James showed him again the 'another six' on the side of his leather boot. "Cricket will always be my first love."

"A deeper love with a cricket bat. You're beyond help."

"I don't need any help. I'm not the one in the friend zone."

"Just trying to form a deeper connection, that's all."

"Sounds like she's playing you around, buddy," James said, appearing to care for Ethan.

Ethan was fine with his progress, but compared to James's success rate, he did sense he was in the slow lane and should speed up to get some long-awaited action with Rachel.

James convinced Ethan they should go out again on the following Thursday. "If you play a little hard to get, she'll be begging for it."

"Suppose you're right." Ethan hadn't agreed to go out with Rachel until Friday, as she was out with some work mates to celebrate the big sale. "Okay. We're on."

* * *

Thursday night came and after starting out with a few drinks at the local, Ethan and James went to the Red Lion in town. Ethan certainly felt more confident, and James had noticed it. "I think you're ready to be a proper wingman."

Ethan shook his head at James's juvenile tone. After another couple of pints, James pointed out two girls dancing together. They moved to the edge of the dance floor and James gestured for them to join him and Ethan for drinks. Much to Ethan's astonishment they came, James got some drinks and returned to the bar for a round of shots. Getting out with James and Rachel had certainly given Ethan more confidence and he chatted comfortably with them whilst James was at the bar. He teased them a little as Jenny and Jules had a bit of a double act ring to it. They played up to it and did a little tango pose for him.

When James returned, he slipped in between them, putting his arm around Jenny with Jules, then putting her arm around Ethan. They all took their shots together and Jules kissed Ethan on the cheek. He glanced at James, who was already snogging away with Jenny. He then followed suit and took Jules in his arms, delivering gentle kisses to her neck. She moaned and with both hands grabbed his hair and pulled his lips to hers. He responded by planting his hands on her cute round bum.

James interrupted them. "Come on! We're going." Before Ethan could blink, Jules had dragged him along and they were all in a taxi heading for James's place.

Once at James's, he led Jenny directly upstairs, leaving Ethan and Jules in his small lounge. Jules jumped into Ethan's arms and flung her legs around him to launch into a frenzied kiss. Ethan was still catching up. The effect of the beers had clouded his judgement. Ethan rested Jules down on the sofa and she tried to pull him on top of her, but he stepped back. She was oblivious and concentrated on removing her top.

Ethan wanted to be with Rachel, but he also wanted sex and with the perfect tits of Jules being revealed to him, a carnal message switched on in his head. He went down to his knees and placed his face between her luscious breasts, whilst Jules turned her attention to unbuttoning Ethan's shirt.

If Ethan went with the flow as James had put it, he'd be back in the game, but it wasn't the game Ethan wanted to play. He sat back on his heels and put his hand on hers, stopping her descent down his shirt. He stood and re-buttoned his shirt. "Sorry. I need to get going. Got an early start tomorrow."

"I'm at work in the morning, too. I wasn't planning an all-night session," she said, stretching out her hands towards him and following him to the door.

"I really must go." He awkwardly peeled off her hands and opened the front door. "I'll call you Monday for a proper date." He had no intention of calling her, but it felt like the right thing to say.

"Don't bother," she said, as she slammed the door behind him.

Back home, Ethan reflected that perhaps he'd been too slow with Rachel, but she was a much classier girl than Jules and would make a better long-term option.

Chapter 7

The following morning, Ethan was feeling guilty for running out on them and gave James a call.

"Julie and Jules are still here." Jeers from them both confirmed it. "They're staying for breakfast." James moved to another room to speak more freely. "Ethan! You don't owe Rachel anything, you're only mates."

"It just didn't feel right."

"I can't believe you, you're a single bloke and a bird has got her tits out for you. You need your head examining." He sighed. "I'm wondering if you're past help."

"You've been a big help, but I'm going to hold out for Rachel," Ethan said, laying himself wide open to ridicule.

"I think you've lost the plot. Come out again tonight. I won't rest till I've got you laid." Although James had his choice of women, he clearly still wanted the companionship of Ethan. Maybe it was just to share his stories of scoring, but he wasn't ready to let Ethan bail on him.

"I'm supposed to be out with Rachel tonight."

"Is she your new best buddy? I told you. You're in the friend zone. Unless you're happy with pretty little kisses, you need to drop her and come get yourself some pussy with me. Or are you nervous about showing a girl your little dick?" James said with a taunting tease.

Ethan could sense James's desperation to keep his new wingman in tow and smiled. "My dick's big enough. I'm trying to build a relationship with Rachel. Have you ever thought about finding a classy bird to click with?"

"Not interested in the friend zone. Do you realise Rachel has probably got another guy on the go and you're her little toy to tease on a Monday night?"

"I'm seeing her tonight," Ethan said, before shaking his head at the confirmed bachelor. Ethan ended the call with his head clear. He was taking the traditional courtship route and planned to make steady progress with Rachel.

After the call, Ethan convinced himself that Rachel was more than a mate and she definitely wouldn't be seeing another guy. Ethan was also proud of himself for not taking the offer of sex from Jules. He sat back on his sofa, proud to wait for Rachel.

Mid-afternoon, his phone rang.

"Sorry Ethan, I can't make it tonight. One of my colleagues is leaving, and the boss is treating us to a night out."

The term pride before a fall came to mind. He drowned his sorrows in some beers. Not wanting to stay home on a Friday night, a dejected Ethan rang James prepared for ridicule. "She's put me off till Monday."

Ethan held the phone away from his ear as raucous laughter boomed out of the phone. When it calmed, he returned the phone to his ear.

"I told you. You're wasting your time with her. If they don't jump in the sack by a third date, they're just teasing you."

"I don't think that's completely true."

"I suppose a few religious nuts may hold off longer, but that's what I've found. Hold off on the first date and go for it on the second. Some play hard to get, but if they're holding off on the third date, forget it and move on."

"Are you out tonight?" Ethan asked.

"Sure am. I'll pick you up at nine. We can go straight to the Red Lion."

"How about the Groove?"

"Think we're better off in the Lion. They're younger and fitter."

"Don't you think it's time to move on from the younger women."

"Not just yet. Older women will swallow you up. You need to train on the younger, more impressionable. They're more fun, anyway."

"I suppose a bit more training would help." Ethan rolled his eyes at James's persuasive antics.

"You leavin' your mobile at home again?" James said.

"Was going to, why?"

"Think your method for collecting numbers is risky. Write your number on your hand. At least they'll be able to call you. You can easily block their calls after you've had 'em."

* * *

Crestfallen, with his number written on his palm, Ethan was ready to seek a new partner. James was on form again and with Ethan in tow, they chatted to a couple of young girls who looked fresh out of college. James started popping jokes about the bed in his flat being big enough for four, and Ethan was cringing. It wasn't what Ethan wanted. He wanted Rachel. He enjoyed taking things slowly.

"We're good friends. We don't mind sharing." James said with a grin towards Ethan. Ethan held back, rolling his eyes and excused himself to leave them giggling away. He headed upstairs to where he'd sat with Rachel. Ethan needed five minutes to collect his thoughts. He wasn't comfortable with James and his "go with the flow" routine, but wasn't confident enough to head out on his own.

Ethan took an abrupt halt when he reached the booths and spotted Rachel laughing with a couple of well-dressed guys. He thought she was cheating on him until he remembered she was out with work. Another two girls were squished into the same booth with an older guy,

With everyone else moving, and him rooted like a statue. It drew eyes to him, especially Rachel's. She waved her hand to beckon him over as she shouted in true leary style, "Ethan, come over here!"

She was off her face as she introduced everyone from the office and introduced Ethan as "her new boyfriend." Ethan wished James had been there to see it. The relationship was definitely on and held more appeal than James and a couple of impressionable youngsters.

The eldest guy stood and offered Ethan a seat. "I'm off now. Good to meet you, Ethan. Look after her. She's a wonderful lady and my best saleswoman." Ethan accepted his firm handshake and did likewise with the other guys as they climbed out of the booth. The other girls went with them, giving both Ethan and Rachel a cute wave.

No sooner were they out of sight, Rachel pulled Ethan in close and planted a drunken, yet passionate kiss on his lips. Ethan reciprocated, and their hands caressed each other. A firework display of senses exploded through Ethan as she reached between his legs. He slid his hand up the inside of her leg, but an interruption came with one of the polite droids beeping with increasing volume until they came up for air.

"No heavy petting," the one metre tall security droid boomed with a display on its chest screen, which confirmed its instruction. Sniggers from a few onlookers made it an embarrassing intrusion.

Rachel sat up like a prissy church girl before she burst into a fit of giggles and suggested to Ethan, "shall we go to yours?"

Ethan needed no further prompting. He took her hand with a positive, "let's go," and pulled Rachel all the way to the taxi rank. Her lips returned to his for their short ride to Ethan's.

Who needs James Walker? Ethan thought as he took her hand to lead her up the stairs to his flat. As he opened the door, Rachel sped past him. "Need the loo."

Whilst she popped to the toilet, Ethan grabbed the clothes strewn about and did a quick tidy up job in his bedroom.

He headed to the bathroom door. "Are you okay in there?"

"Can you make coffee?" she pleaded through the door.

"No prob."

"Black, no sugar. Please."

Rachel was still in the bathroom when he'd poured the coffee. Not wanting to be too presumptuous, he took the coffees into the lounge rather than the bedroom. "Coffee's ready!"

"Okay!" a tired croak returned. She didn't sound like she was still partying and thoughts of her appearing stripped ready for action disappeared.

Another minute and a sheepish, bedraggled Rachel skulked out of the bathroom.

"Did you throw up?" Ethan asked with all the kindness of a bachelor.

"Too much to drink," Rachel replied in a sorrowful voice, as she sat on the other end of the sofa.

"Why didn't you take a sober pill?"

"Didn't plan on drinking so much."

"Shall I get you one?" Ethan said, as he passed her the mug of coffee and stroked her leg. She brushed his hand away and uttered a feeble whimper, "I just need coffee."

Chapter 8

After another non-starter with Rachel, Ethan rang his college buddy, Mirek, for some of his wisdom, but got no reply. With nobody else to turn to, Ethan rang James Walker for more tainted advice. Not that Mirek was a saint.

"Told you to ditch her. She's a waste of time unless you want to end up in a serious relationship."

"That's exactly what I want!"

James huffed. "As her platonic friend."

"No."

"You've seen her three times, and she keeps slapping you away." James laughed to himself. "I bet she's said she finds you really easy to talk to."

Ethan was about to reply that she had, but James continued, "You're her new buddy. Every time she gets shafted by a bloke she'll call you up, hug you and tell you she wishes all guys were like you before she goes out with another player."

"Like you?" Ethan said as he rolled his eyes.

"Exactly." James replied like it wasn't a criticism. "Listen Ethan, forget about her. We'll get you laid tonight. Saturday nights are a dead cert. No work in the morning, so they'll be drunk and ripe for it." James didn't give Ethan chance to reply, "I'll pick you up at eight," with that he ended the call with

Ethan's mouth agape.

He threw his phone onto the sofa. James had told Ethan to move on from Rachel, but he didn't want to. Ethan wanted to wait until she was ready, but he couldn't disagree with James. She had messed with his emotions, but he still preferred her company to James's. She was a better option than being thrust into James's seeded conveyor belt of easy and gullible women.

"Let's try to get this moving," Ethan announced as he grabbed his mobile to message Rachel. As he began the message, his phone rang.

"Hiya. Sorry about last night. Had too much to drink," Rachel said.

"When did you leave?" Ethan asked.

"I woke up at five, didn't want to wake you. I needed to show another house at eleven and needed to get home and shower."

"It's okay. Did you get another sale?"

"Waste of time. It was a young couple who hadn't even got enough for a deposit. Got another guy viewing it on Monday. Hopefully, I'll be able to close the deal with him."

It sounded like she'd be prepared to use more than her professional charm, and the thought of her seducing him dropped into Ethan's head.

Rachel broke into his mental argument. "Are you still there?"

He shook his head. James was tainting his mind. Rachel wouldn't do that. "I'm still here."

"Would you like to come around for a film tonight? Need to give the drink a rest, besides Saturday night is full of predators and slappers."

Not wrong there, he thought. "Won't Brad and your mom be there?"

"We can go to my dad's. I often stay there weekends to get

49

away from Brad's antics. Don't worry, my dad will be out with his mates. Come around at seven."

Sorted.

Ethan had trouble holding back his smile when he called James. "Can't make tonight. Rachel has asked me to go around for Netflix and Chill at seven."

"Seven! She's probably going to sell you the property. When she kicks you out at nine, join me at the club. See you later." He ended the call.

James had put the phone down on him again. Ethan stared at the phone, shaking his head.

Rachel's dad's house was a modest semi-detached with a Tesla outside. Ethan gave the door a confident knock and heard her dashing downstairs. She opened the door with a breathy, "Hi," before she turned away from him and plumped up a cushion on the sofa. "Great timing. My dad has just gone. Did you eat yet? Shall I order a pizza?"

"Pizza? Sounds like a plan." He said with a calmness, which belied the nervousness that had bitten him on his stroll to the house. She had called him her boyfriend, she'd invited him round, but the comments from James had removed his eager anticipation. He planned to go with the flow. If they were to remain platonic friends, then so be it. It was better than playing along with James's crazy no plan, plan. "What time's your dad back?" he said, as he took a seat on the sofa.

"He's out drinking with his buddies won't be back until the early hours. We've got the night to ourselves," she said with a confident smile as she dropped onto the seat beside him.

Rachel had dressed for a relaxing night with joggers and a hoody. It hid some of her shape, but from the dress she wore on their last date, he knew she was reasonably trim. He was not one to complain, as his indulgence in beers and fast food had given him the cuddle factor.

Rachel asked him more about his work, whilst she tapped their pizza request into her phone. Ethan was proud to announce his boss had mentioned sending him on a trip to New York. "It's not for a few weeks, but I'll learn more about robotics."

Rachel tilted her head and pursed her lips. "Not leaving me already, are you?"

Ethan smiled at her pining pose. "Not yet. We've got plenty of time. It'll only be for four weeks."

He'd finally got close to Rachel and now he'd revealed he wouldn't be around, but thankfully unmoved by his rambling, Rachel leant her head against his chest like he'd told her he'd always be there for her.

He gave her a gentle kiss on the top of her head, and she lifted her head for him to feel her warm lips on his. "Are you not bothered about me going away for a month?" As soon as he'd said it, he wanted to punch himself in the face. Was he trying to ruin this before it begun?

"You're ambitious and the robotics knowledge may get you a job with the Tushi Corporation. As long as you behave yourself." She stared with intent, her dark brown eyes burning into his. "I get very jealous."

Where it came from, he didn't know, but he spurted an attempt at singing, with a song lyric from his mom's collection. "I only have eyes for you."

Rachel responded like a light switched on after an eternity in the darkness, her full lips meeting his and her legs moving astride him. If he could have continued singing, he would have gone into heaven. I'm in heaven.

His arousal grew, and he pulled her body close to his to feel her sweet breasts against his chest. She nibbled his ear and whispered, "that was to stop you singing."

Rachel wriggled out of his tickling grasp and gave him a focused stare as she stepped back to remove her joggers and reveal the cutest white cotton panties he could have hoped to see. She let him take in the sight of her before she said, "get your pants off then." She then knelt down before him and frantically pulled at his trousers, helping to remove them as Ethan wriggled on the sofa.

"Is this too early? We haven't known each other long," she asked.

"It's fine," Ethan uttered as he leant forward and pulled her back onto the sofa beside him. "Where were we?" he said with a cheeky smile as he leant into her and delivered kisses to her neck as he took in her now familiar vanilla scent.

"You won't cheat on me, will you?" She asked nervously. "When you're in America."

"I won't cheat on you anywhere," Ethan said. He slipped his hands to her waist and danced kisses across her toned stomach. She lay back on the arm of the sofa and stretched her arms over her head.

Working his way up the side of her stomach, he lifted her top to reveal a matching cotton bra holding her delicate breasts. She helped and pulled her hoody over her head and flung it away. Ethan's lips delicately danced up to her breasts. She turned her head away for him to nibble her neck and when he did; she moaned her appreciation.

"Have you taken a neutralise pill?" she asked.

Ethan had heard about the neutralise pills. James took one every day, but with Ethan's activity level, neutralising his sperm had not been necessary. "No. Got a condom in my wallet, though. I think it's still in date." Ethan cursed himself. Why didn't he just scream out he was inexperienced?

Her breath became guttural, like someone possessed, and she impatiently growled, "put it on then!"

He grabbed his discarded trousers and grabbed the crumpled little packet and ripped it open. Rachel impeded his attempt at placing it over his dick by trying to pull his shirt over his head. "You'll have to undo the buttons," he said.

"No, I won't," she insisted and with a strong desire, she pulled at his shirt to pop the buttons off.

"Or not," he said, catching her passionate and possibly possessed stare.

Another pull, and his shirt opened to reveal his portly stomach. Her nails dug into his chest, and she gently nibbled his nipple. "It's time," she said with a heavy breath.

With condom suitably in place, he pulled off the rest of his shirt and took in Rachel as she lay back waiting for him to make love to her. He slid his hands along the outside of her thighs and over her petite rear to pull her panties off. She helped before sitting up to launch her tongue into his mouth and her hands pulled at his hair. Far from being painful, it was the most erotic experience he'd ever had, not that he'd had many.

Ethan lowered her back onto the sofa, and his sturdy frame settled on her. Her head tilted back over the arm of the sofa as he nibbled at her exposed, slender neck. Her hand reached around to find Ethan's erection and she guided it to where she wanted it. Ethan slowly connected with her and an explosion of senses rippled through him.

Knock! Knock!

They both froze.

"Pizza!" a gruff voice hollered from behind the door.

"Leave it on the mat!" Rachel shouted, before pulling Ethan back down to kiss her.

The love of a beautiful woman wanting him and needing him excited him, with sensations switching on every light in Ethan's mind and body. He wanted to enjoy every second with this wild demon that had taken over Rachel's body, but his manhood had other ideas and was ready to shoot. All his focus was on trying to last longer, but she trembled with each steady thrust and the pent-up pressure inside him grew and grew.

She was certainly enjoying it as much as he was, but with his lack of sexual activity, his peak arrived with a judder of both satisfaction and disappointment. He held himself inside her, but his lack of movement told her the show was over and her hand reached between them for her to finish her part of the deal. Ethan enjoyed the intense focus on her face as she reached her climax and flung her arms back around him.

Thoughts of the pizza outside called him, but he resisted as he waited for her to come down from her high and let calm Rachel back in the room.

"Okay, get off me now. The pizza's getting cold." She said with her normal voice returning.

* * *

James called the following morning. "Did you buy the property?" He asked in a cheery tone.

Ethan laughed. "Kind of."

"Did my coaching work, then?"

"What coaching?" Ethan replied.

"I knew if I said you were in the friend zone, you'd finally push it with her and close the deal."

"Didn't quite happen like that."

"Oh, my God! She jumped you, didn't she?" James said with an almost disbelieving tone that Ethan had made a breakthrough.

Ethan smirked to himself. "Sort of."

"That's the first stage of your training complete. Now you need to close the deal on your own."

"I did after the film."

"You dirty dog. Twice in one night after a five-year dry spell. You're definitely back in the game."

"Okay, it had been a while, but it's not a game for me."

"I guess you stayed the night?"

"Nah, her dad was due back."

"Or her other bloke?"

"Not everyone is cheating and lying. Some people just want to find a partner."

"Boring! She'll be inviting you round to meet her dad next. Avoid it. If he knows you've been getting some from his daughter, he'll probably chop your dick off."

"She's not some impressionable young woman and from what I found out last night, she's not so naïve."

"I hope it lasts." The joking tone in James's voice mellowed to a moment of sincerity. "Sounds like you've found a good woman. Good luck to you. I knew you weren't for the crazy life like me, but it was fun to have you as a wingman for a while. I suppose you won't want to come out with me anymore now you've got yourself a girly-friend. That's what all the others did."

"I won't ditch you, you helped to get me out and about again.

55

I wouldn't have met Rachel, if not for you. I'm up for going out, but I won't be unfaithful to Rachel."

Chapter 9

"We need to get up. The video screens will be here soon," Rachel said, trying to stir Ethan from his bed.

"What are you talking about?" his sleepy response.

"To brighten up the lounge. The floral garden."

"Come back to bed."

"You had enough last night. It's time to get up." She pulled the duvet off the bed and headed to his kitchen. "I'll make coffee. Get dressed!"

Rachel had ordered the screens after receiving a sizeable bonus and was putting another of her stamps on Ethan's place.

The installers arrived on time and took less than ten minutes to unroll the screens along the wall and secure them to bring a beautiful garden to life in his apartment.

Ethan marvelled at the vibrant live display. "These must have cost a fortune."

"The place needed brightening up. Anyway, don't worry, we can move them when we get our own place. A few more bonus cheques and you getting a job at Tushi should do it."

"Tushi," Ethan sighed. "Need to get the boss to come good on the robotics training first."

"Cream always rises to the top. It'll happen."

Ethan thanked Rachel for her support, and they arranged

to meet for lunch at Robolicious, a trendy bar run by service droids.

Discussions about their long-term future gave Ethan strength. James would have wanted to run for the hills. He was still picking up new prey every week, with Ethan playing the unwilling sidekick whenever James convinced him to venture out. Ethan would've preferred to stay home when Rachel was working or taking her grandma knitting, but James was very persuasive, droning on about how Ethan wouldn't have met Rachel if not for his encouragement and advice.

On the occasions Ethan joined James, Ethan didn't want to ruin James's chances by rebuffing girls on the spot, instead he collected phone numbers before he put them down softly the following day. It became a guilty pleasure for Ethan after years of struggling to attract women. He enjoyed batting them off to stay true to Rachel.

Ethan's boss had promised him a trip to New York for advanced robotics training, but Ethan thought it was a carrot he'd never get to taste. When he met Rachel for lunch at Robolicious, things took a turn for the better. They'd been there before, but on this occasion, one of the server droids dropped their tray of food on its way to their table.

Jeers rang out in derision for the place. Finlay, the faultless looking tanned owner, darted around from his comfortable perch. "I'm sorry guys, these things should to be error free but they're costing me a fortune in lost business. I'll get you some free drinks whilst I get a replacement for your meal. There'll be no charge."

"Can't you fix them." Rachel said, nudging Ethan.

Finlay's eyes opened wide. He glared at Ethan like he had the glow of an angel around him.

Ethan had fixed some house bots and service droids, but robot vacuum cleaners were his regular work. With his renewed confidence and the prod from Rachel, he said, "I could look for you. I've fixed one or two."

"He fixes them all the time," Rachel said, giving Ethan a further nudge.

"Can you have a look?" he pleaded. "Free food and drink for life if you can stop them ruining my business."

Ethan turned back to Rachel and gave her a winning smile. He took the service droid into the back and meticulously checked the circuitry. The pristine looking, yet dim, Finlay had a diagnostic kit but had never read up on how to use it. It was second nature to Ethan. He checked over the service droid and made the necessary adjustments before calibrating each movement.

When Ethan returned to find Rachel, she'd already eaten and returned to work.

"Sorry mate, she left about ten minutes ago. Can you check over the rest?" Finlay asked.

"Need to get back to work. I'll be back with a service agreement later."

"Thought you were happy with eating for free."

"We've already established I'd be eating and drinking here for free, but I need to speak to my boss and arrange a longer-term service contract."

"Knew it would cost me." Finlay tutted as if Ethan had robbed him.

"I thought it was the faulty droids that were costing you." Ethan said as he headed off.

* * *

59

Ethan's boss rubbed his hands together, delighted with the extra business. Prompted by Ethan, he agreed to set up Ethan's trip to New York. Ethan also negotiated a cut of the profit from the service contract. The time spent with James had helped Ethan. He'd become a more positive force. Rachel tried to claim the credit for giving him the nudge he needed, but she couldn't deny Ethan was the tech genius.

With the New York trip approaching, Ethan and Rachel used their time together well, including another visit to Robolicious. Finlay kept to his word and treated them like royalty. Life for Ethan was definitely on the up. He wanted to celebrate. "Let's go on a spa break this weekend. We can celebrate my boss finally coming good on his promise, not to mention the bonus cheque I've got coming."

A sheepish Rachel bowed her head, "Can't this weekend, meant to mention it before I've got a long weekend planned in Manchester. I'm due to show a house to a billionaire." Ethan leant back and frowned. "Not jealous are you," she teased. "I could be his trophy wife and live a life of leisure."

Ethan leant forward and stroked his chin as a smile grew. "Plenty of commission?"

"If I clinch the deal, my commission will be enough to buy a place for us." She pulled him close and delivered a lingering kiss to his cheek.

Ethan's face glowed, both with the mention of a large commission cheque and Rachel talking about them living together. Ethan grinned. "Are you taking the tight red dress?"

"I'll wear my power suit. No need to fret." She tapped her finger on his nose, smiled and made a sizzling noise as she touched her butt.

Ethan pulled her in for a hug and nibbled on her neck.

"Not here. Wait till tonight," she said.

* * *

"I'll be good. Make sure you are," Rachel said. She'd also suggested, "you should go out for a drink with James, you've not seen him for a while."

Ethan didn't share the reason.

James turned down a pint at the local and insisted they should have a proper night out before Rachel had him married with kids. James painted the image of being married with kids as a bad thing, but it fit perfectly with what Ethan had in mind.

If James had been a regular guy, Ethan would have discussed how he planned to propose to Rachel, but James would've simply dismissed it as missing out on all the other available women.

Ethan hadn't wanted to feel jealous, but with James nagging at his ear about the possibility of the billionaire taking his Rachel, he became increasingly worried.

They put the club on hold for the Red Lion. Ethan picked it as it was a relaxed place where people stopped off after work and had fewer young women who'd throw themselves at any bloke after a couple of drinks.

Ethan hoped an early start would mean an early finish to avoid the pairing up that occurred in the early hours. When Ethan arrived and spotted James through the crowd, he already had a couple of other guys, plus four women huddled around him. Three of the girls were in power suits after a hard slog in the office, but the fourth, Emma, wore a figure-hugging orange dress which presented her ample breasts like candy in a shop window.

The short redhead laughed at James's jokes and held onto Ethan's arm to stop herself from toppling over on her heels.

Emma was a pocket rocket of a girl and repeatedly rested her head against his shoulder, like they were a couple. When the two guys headed off with two of the power suited women, it left Ethan and James with Emma and her colleague, Trudy.

Trudy was much taller and wore the trouser suit well. She'd taken a shine to James's crass style and began snapping selfies with him. "Let's get us all in," she said. Ethan put his arm around Emma as they huddled together for the pic.

"You girls joining us in the club?" James asked, with Ethan snapping his head towards James.

Trudy and Emma exchanged a glance before making their apologies and heading together to the ladies' room.

"Looks like we're on." James beamed. "Emma looks like a right little firecracker."

Ethan's expression was plain as he slowly shook his head. "I'm not going to the club. I'm going home."

"You're kidding, right?"

"No. I'm happy with Rachel."

"You'd better not fuck this up for me. I thought about what you said about settling down and I think Trudy could be the one for me."

"I'm not interested in Emma."

"If Rachel falls for the billionaire and doesn't come back. What are you going to do?"

"She'll be back and if she sells the house, we'll be moving in together. I don't want to fuck it up. Rachel's the one for me. I love her. I want to marry her."

James let out a heavy sigh. "Listen to me. You don't have to do anything you don't want to, but just stay out so I can find out if Trudy could be something special for me. I helped you get Rachel."

Ethan sighed.

"Play it nice and easy tonight with Emma and get her number. If Rachel goes off with the billionaire, you can give Emma a call. If not, forget it."

"Okay. You owe me, though."

"No worries. You'll be fine." James shook his hand, agreement complete.

Ethan's discomfort eased when Trudy was making her way through the crowd without Emma.

"Problem solved. I'm off home," Ethan said to James, but the words stuck in his mouth when Emma appeared from behind Trudy.

"Not going home, are you?" she asked with a frown.

"No. He's with us. Come on Ethan," James replied on his behalf and took Trudy by the hand to lead them to the club.

* * *

The drinks flowed in the club. Ethan's head throbbed. With James and Trudy set for the night. Ethan figured it was his time for an exit. "My head's pounding," he said to Emma.

Emma put a caring hand on his shoulder. "Shall we go somewhere quieter? The lounger's upstairs are comfy."

"I'm going home."

"Shall I come with you?"

"Not a great idea. I'll probably throw up at some point. Not pleasant."

"I'll look after you."

"It's okay."

"Thought you liked me."

"I do, it's just I need to get home." Ethan stood to leave.

"You've not even asked for my number." Her face was like a child deprived of sweets.

"I don't have a mobile with me."

"Give me yours." Primed with her finger over her mobile.

Rachel's influence had meant he'd now memorised his number. If he changed the last two digits, he'd appease her and leave. He rattled off the number. Shit. He'd not changed the last two numbers.

Emma was suitably pleased and snapped a quick pic to put aside his number. "I've messaged you. Drop one back to let me know you're home okay."

"No worries." Ethan left James sucking face with Trudy, whilst Emma was tapping something else into her phone. Ethan figured if Rachel got taken in by the billionaire, he now had an option. Emma was kinda cute.

His phone had two messages when he got home. Sadly, neither were from Rachel. The first was as described by Emma and the second, "Thanks for an enjoyable night. See you soon X."

He popped a message back. "Thanks for a good night. X"

Chapter 10

A game of cricket on Sunday morning provided a welcome distraction from waiting to hear from Rachel. He'd messaged her to join him at the cricket club when she got back. He even took his mobile with him to check for any response.

James failed to mention he'd invited Trudy and Emma. When they appeared, Ethan immediately regretted messaging Rachel and hoped her distaste for watching cricket was greater than how much she'd missed him. The last thing he wanted was an appearance from Rachel, with Emma hanging around. After a fruitless over, he returned to deep field and Emma walked around the field to chat with him.

"Shame you had to run off last night. Was I too forward for you?"

Ethan didn't turn around to acknowledge her. "Kinda. Thought we'd get to know each other first."

"Did you miss Church to play cricket?"

Ethan laughed and glanced around to see her playful grin before returning his focus to the game.

"You're different. You've got more about you than most. I don't mind waiting for you to be ready," Emma said.

Ethan turned around again to see her heading back towards

the pavilion. He was sure she was waggling her pert butt deliberately.

She glanced around and gave him a pearly white smile when she caught him looking. "I'm looking forward to Monday. Shall we meet at seven?"

"I'll call you," Ethan said, although he'd no intention of calling, unless Rachel had decided she preferred Mr. Manchester.

His team secured victory thanks to a sterling performance from James at the crease. Drinking occupied the rest of the afternoon. Thankfully, Trudy and Emma had gone, something to do with a new job Trudy was starting on Monday. At the end of every pint, Ethan anxiously checked to see if he'd received contact from Rachel.

He hadn't.

* * *

Ethan headed to work with still no word from Rachel. The likelihood of an ongoing liaison with Mr. Manchester left his head, and he became worried about her safety.

At 10am, his mobile burst into life. "Did you miss me?" The bright and cheery Rachel asked.

"Was worried, I hadn't heard from you."

"Devon insisted on taking me out for lunch after the viewing, to confirm the deal. He invited me to a party, and I went along with it."

"Sounds awful." Ethan rolled his eyes, waiting for the kick in the balls at how Devon was irresistible.

"He tried to get me into bed! When I told him to get lost, he backed out of the deal and I lost my 40k commission. I didn't call because I was in a rotten mood. I went back to the hotel and cleared the minibar instead."

"Expensive," Ethan said, his eyes wide with surprise and relief at how she'd rebuffed the jerk to stay true to him.

"He'd covered the accommodation."

"Nice move." Ethan laughed.

"Not really. My head spun, and I threw up before I could get to the bathroom."

"You should have taken me with you and shared the drinking. Are you okay now?"

"My head is still pounding, but I've just taken a sober pill."

"Why didn't you take one last night?"

"If I wasn't so pissed, I would've done," she snapped.

Ethan smiled to himself. "I was expecting you back yesterday."

"I slept right through Sunday and woke up at five this morning. Got the first hyper-loop back."

"That's what you call sleeping it off. You wanna come to mine later?"

"Got a bright-eyed starter shadowing me all day. I said we'd have drinks after work, but I don't fancy it now. Could you save me about seven?"

"No problem." Ethan smiled.

"I haven't got an appointment until Tuesday afternoon. I could stay at yours if you like."

"Sounds like a plan," Ethan said as he rested back against the sofa. Rachel was with him for the long haul.

Late afternoon, Ethan got a surprise call from a delighted Rachel. "The dickhead in Manchester has confirmed he wants to go ahead. I've got my commission back."

"That's glorious news. I'm really pleased for you."

"Pleased for me? Don't you mean pleased for us. We can get the house now."

"What house?"

"I've had my eye on it for a couple of weeks. A semi-detached near town. If you get the afternoon off, I can give you a private viewing." The fun in her voice had Ethan's balls tingling with anticipation. "You want to move in together, don't you?"

"Of course, I do. You're my world." Ethan had hoped they'd move in together. It was sooner than he thought, but he loved her. "Can you ditch your trainee for a couple of hours, have an extended private viewing."

"Couple of hours. Will you need that long?" She giggled down the phone.

"Send me the address. Shall I meet you there about three?"

"Two is good. Give me a chance to go home and change. I did some lingerie shopping in Manchester."

Ethan adjusted his semi-erect tackle before he knocked on his boss's door. Still in his boss's good books, he granted him the afternoon off, in exchange for a Saturday morning of minding the trade desk.

* * *

As the taxi rolled into Lament Lane, Ethan wondered who had given it such a sad name, in such a pleasant area. The taxi stopped outside number 38 and, like a light being turned on, the sun shone onto the front of the house. This was surely the place to make a home. He stepped out of the taxi. The warmth of the summer sun on his back perfected his dream sequence. This could be the place to bring up a family with Rachel. He put his previous relationship woes behind him to mentally dance towards his destiny.

Rachel opened the front door and welcomed him with a firm, business-like handshake. "Good afternoon. Ethan isn't it."

He nodded with a smile before taking her in his arms and giving her the strongest of hugs. After engaging in a lasting kiss, she stepped back into work mode and treated him like any other client.

She led him into the living/dining room, detailing the options for the spacious room leading to the conservatory. A sizeable garden featured an apple tree and decorated borders. A newly fitted kitchen had a full suite of appliances and was a good size.

Rachel didn't crack a smile as she maintained the utmost professionalism giving him the tour, but as she climbed the stairs ahead of Ethan, he got a glimpse of what was to come. Ethan noticed lace stockings under her business suit trousers. Halfway up the stairs, she stopped and turned back to Ethan with half her blouse buttons open to reveal a cool blue lace bra to match the stockings. "You are going to love the bedroom." Her temptress smile turned away and continued to the landing. Ethan's mouth watered for the delights to come. Rachel opened the bathroom door to a Grecian blue tiled wet room with a walk-in shower. She dragged her teeth over her bottom lip and reached out to Ethan with a cat-like claw. "Purr-fect for cooling off."

Ethan's chest heaved, and the bulge in his pants grew. Rachel opened the door to the master bedroom. A blood orange glow from the light shining through the curtains filled the room. Rachel's tone deepened, "I'm feeling hot." She slipped off her blazer and Ethan took her into his arms, pushing her against the wall. He buried his face in her cleavage as she struggled to

69

unbutton the rest of her blouse. Pulling his face to hers, her swollen lips met his, sending tingles throughout his body.

Ethan helped her out of her suit trousers to reveal her lace panties and garter set holding her thigh length stockings.

The floor wasn't ideal, but it was the most passionate sex he'd ever experienced. Not that he had a massive back catalogue, but he knew nothing could eclipse that afternoon.

* * *

Sharing a shower together with Ethan lathering every contour of her body drew a perfect line under their afternoon. Rachel headed back to work to set the paperwork in motion for their first house together as Ethan headed home. After numerous jerks messing her around, she'd finally found someone she could settle down with. After totally ignoring any contraception, if it was meant to be, they might even start a family straight away.

Rachel had discussed with Ethan the possibility of a family in the future, but getting married first was the right route to take. Her shadow for the day immediately called her out when she returned. "You look like you've been having sexy time."

Rachel couldn't deny it and took pleasure in sharing the delights of the private viewing with the bubbly new hire. Rachel took her advice not to regret her fun time and popped to the chemist for a morning-after pill on the way to the bar.

When the others from the office joined them, they were still talking about the guy who'd rocked Rachel's world. Having not met the rest of the team, Rachel introduced Trudy.

Trudy was all smiles and told them, "Rachel has been telling me about her fella. Looks like wedding bells aren't far away."

"Does Ethan know yet?" her boss said, shaking his head and smiling at their excitement.

"Not yet." Rachel laughed, but stopped when Trudy's face went cold. "What's the matter? Are you okay?"

"It's nothing," she waved to Emma, "I've just seen my friend. I'll tell her I'm with you guys tonight."

"Rubbish! She can join us." Rachel said, waving to the little redhead.

Trudy dipped her head, fearing the worst.

Chapter 11

Trudy briefly introduced Emma to her new co-workers and insisted on pulling Emma away for a chat in the ladies' room. Trudy held Emma's shoulders and gave her a panicked stare. "Rachel is about to move in with a guy called Ethan."

"That's a co-incidence. My guy's Ethan too." Emma smiled, completely missing the point.

"It better not be the same one. I don't want my new supervisor finding out my mate has been shagging her bloke."

"I've not been shagging him. Yet. My Ethan is no player. I don't think he's got it in him to play away." She pushed Trudy's arms off and looked at her through the restroom mirror. "You're worrying about nothing. Ethan's not like James."

"What do you mean, not like James?"

"You're blind to it. James is a typical one-night-stand kinda guy."

"He's meeting me here later." Trudy bobbed her tongue out at her long-time buddy.

"I bet he doesn't show." Emma stared, awaiting a wager.

Trudy had fallen for the same type of guy many times and knew Emma was probably right. "Enough about James, just don't mention Ethan."

Emma held her hands up in submission. "Okay. If you insist." Emma's lips curled up. "If you get the drinks in."

"Okay, drinks are on me."

* * *

Ethan called James to see if he wanted to join him and Rachel at the bar to check out her work colleagues. He also wanted to check when the next get together was happening with the cricket crew. Since Ethan and Rachel had hit it off, he'd seen little of James, but thought it unfair to drop him because he was in a relationship. Yes, in a relationship. Ethan could hardly believe it himself.

With no answer from James, Ethan assumed he'd moved onto his next conquest. He left a voicemail and headed into the shower.

* * *

The drinks were flowing in the bar, and Rachel was on the tipsy side again. She tapped on Emma's shoulder. "I took my boyfriend to look at a house this afternoon and showed him these." She pulled up her trouser leg to show off her cool blue stockings.

"Nice. Did you get the garter set?" Emma asked.

"Yep, and the bra." Rachel popped a blouse button to show a glimpse.

"I've got me one of those," Emma said.

"All for my Ethan," Rachel said with an exaggerated nod.

"I've got me one of those."

"You've got an Ethan too? Snap." Rachel giggled at the connection.

Trudy interjected and put an arm around Emma as she sneered into her eyes, "you've got to be going. Haven't you?"

"Have I?" Emma frowned.

"You should stay. Ethan will be here soon," said Rachel.

"Maybe next time. We need to get going." Trudy grabbed Emma's hand and pulled her to the exit and shoved her directly into an awaiting taxi. "Need to get you home."

As the taxi pulled away, Emma's face shot to the window. "There he is." Ethan was striding confidently into the bar.

* * *

"Ethan!" Rachel called, waving her hand to get his attention.

Ethan spotted her and made his way to her. "Are you drunk again?" Ethan said as he put his arms around her.

"Bit tipsy, that's all." Ignoring her colleagues, she kissed him and ran her fingers through his hair.

Ethan enjoyed the unbridled affection but knew it was likely to end in her throwing up again. "Think I should get you back to mine."

"We've had a delightful time, haven't we?" Rachel said, sweeping her hand around in front of her colleagues. "You should have been here earlier. You've just missed Trudy and her friend Emma. Emma's got an Ethan too." Rachel's rambling stopped. "Are you okay? You look ever so pale."

The realisation hit Ethan like a bat in the face as panic grabbed him. "Let's get going," He took her hand and after a brief apology, Ethan swiftly led Rachel outside. Rachel responded to his positive move and as soon as they were in the taxi, she grabbed his head and pulled his lips to hers. After getting over the relief of a close shave, Ethan enjoyed the attention of his awoken goddess.

Ethan struggled to get his fingerprints to register on the door pad to his flat with Rachel tickling him.

"Why's it not working?" Rachel asked impatiently. "Why don't you just have a key?"

"I don't need a key; I've got my hand." He placed his hand back on the pad and the door opened.

"A key would have been easier." Rachel said, before resuming her tickle of Ethan's waist.

Ethan returned a tickle and Rachel screamed as he pinned her onto the sofa until she announced she needed a wee.

When she returned from the bathroom, Rachel said, "You could rent this out again, help cover the mortgage."

"No more talking shop. I want you on my bed." Excitedly, she darted past him and jumped onto the bed.

"We're going to get a house together. Shall we have babies too?" Her energy and love for Ethan beamed out as she bounced on the bed.

Ethan returned a wide smile. "Love you, even when you're drunk."

"I should hope so," Rachel said, wagging her finger at him.

Joining her standing on the bed. Ethan kissed her before she ushered him off the bed and demanded he sing the stripper tune as she peeled off her jacket. Rachel joined in with the singing as she unbuttoned her blouse and swung it around before launching it at Ethan. She lay down on the bed with her legs aloft as she undid her trousers and slid them off. She made

75

like a star on the bed. "Make love to me," she demanded.

Ethan undressed and stood at the foot of the bed to take in all her beauty. He delicately tantalised her by brushing kisses over her foot and up the inside of her leg. She giggled and wriggled before wrapping her legs around his waist.

* * *

Rachel was awake first. She rested the coffees on the bedside cupboard and tickled his toes before dancing kisses up his leg. Ethan's erection awoke before he did, and when he stirred, her mouth was already consuming him.

"This is the best way to wake up for sure. Hot coffee by my bedside."

Her teeth bit down gently on his shaft as she groaned her annoyance.

He quickly added, "and the love of my life in my bed."

"That's more like it," she said.

"Don't speak with your mouth full," he joked.

He stroked her hair calmly as she continued, but he soon lost control. His legs writhed and his back arched before he exploded his release for her to taste him. Rachel moaned in the pleasure of his obvious delight.

She'd finally found a deeper love, and to please Ethan meant everything to her. Her hands caressed his stomach before she danced kisses up his chest. She lifted her head to take a mental snapshot of the moment before her swollen lips met his and she released her passion for him.

Ethan tingled all over for the love of Rachel. The salty taste in her wet passion filled kisses an instant reminder of her committed desire for him. Her tongue whirled a further sensation of delight he'd never experienced before. He was complete.

Rachel lifted her head again. "Need the loo." She stopped in the door's frame for a second before returning to give him another quick kiss. She tapped her finger on his nose. "Be ready to go again."

Ethan's hands settled behind his head. "This is heaven."

Rachel returned with his mobile in her hand. "It was buzzing. Tell James you're not going anywhere."

Ethan unlocked the phone with Rachel paying close attention. When he saw it wasn't James, he slipped the phone onto the bedside cupboard. "Not important, still not heard from James."

"Who was it?" Rachel asked.

"Probably my mom. I'll pop in to see her later."

Rachel frowned. "I want to see."

Ethan didn't know whose number it was, but he could guess.

"You've gone pale again. Give me your phone," she demanded. Ethan averted his eyes as he reluctantly passed it to her.

Rachel's nostrils flared. "What the fuck?" She read out the message, "Are you seeing Rachel as well as me?"

"It's nothing. She's a looney," Ethan said, screwing a finger to the side of his head.

"There are more messages. This better not be Trudy's friend, Emma." Rachel punched aggressively into the phone for the other messages.

"Trudy met James the other night. Emma hasn't stopped messaging me since."

"No wonder if this was your reply. Thanks for a good night."

A kissing emoji followed it. Rachel exaggerated the Kiss and took a slow, deep breath in. She pursed her lips to release a controlled breath. She was like a coiled spring about to pop.

Ethan needed to talk quick. "Nothing happened. She just came with Trudy to the cricket. I was just being friendly."

"Friendly? Friendly isn't exchanging numbers and kissing."

"It's just an emoji, it means nothing."

"You didn't tell her you were with me? She thinks you're a couple."

"Give me the phone. I'll call her and tell her now."

Rachel continued looking through the messages and then tapped her own message into his phone.

"Rachel! Look at me. I love you."

Ethan rested his hand on her shoulder, but she scooted away and screamed, "don't fucking touch me!"

Rachel's expression was one of stone. "Let me read another message. Enjoyed watching you at the cricket. Kiss! Kiss!" Rachel picked up the coffee and threw it at Ethan. "I thought I could trust you! You were with her whilst I was in Manchester telling a billionaire to piss off so I could be with you!"

"I haven't had sex with her." Ethan's eyes were full, yet Rachel's were dry and her face as calm as a serial killer delivering a final blow.

"Fact one. You gave her your number, which you couldn't remember when we first met. Fact two. You've seen her whilst I was in Manchester. Fact three. You invited her to the cricket."

"James invited them to the cricket." Ethan regretted it as soon as he'd said it.

Rachel grabbed her trousers and slipped them on. She walked around the bed and picked up her blouse.

"I want to be with you," Ethan's tear-filled plea. "Share a

house with you. Start a family with you. I want to marry you."

Rachel pulled on her blouse, her jacket and slipped on her shoes before she spat her response, "a pitiful marriage proposal. Try harder with Emma."

As she headed to the front door, Ethan followed with his hands open wide. "Don't go. We need to talk about this."

Rachel opened the door and turned back to look Ethan up and down with distaste. A tear ran down her cheek. "I loved you. I gave everything of me to you. You'll regret it."

Rachel slammed the door behind her to leave Ethan staring at the door.

"I regret it already," Ethan said as he turned to face the video wall with tears running down his face. Rachel had brought colour into his grey life. He'd do anything to get her back.

* * *

As relentless as the heavy rain, Ethan left message after message for Rachel. He sent twenty a day for three weeks but didn't receive a reply. He called her, but she must have blocked his number. Ethan concealed his number, but she still didn't answer. He called her work but was told she was out and not to call her again. He bought another mobile and called her, but she didn't answer.

The numbness didn't shift.

Ethan called James. Maybe he could help him get Rachel back or just help him move on. There was no reply. He left another message but didn't get a call back.

A knock on his door brought a moment of optimism, but it crushed any hopes of a reconciliation with Rachel as the

79

installers removed the video wall to leave Ethan once again in darkness.

A week later and Ethan still had no reply from Rachel or James. Ethan knew what James would say when he eventually spoke to him. If you can't be with Rachel, then Emma could be an option for a while to get you going again.

Ethan called Emma but got no reply. He messaged her, "need to talk."

Checking through his phone, he found the message that Rachel must have sent from his phone to Emma. "I'll send you his dick on a plate."

Chapter 12

Ethan dropped his folks off at the airport for their two-week trip to Spain. "Are you sure you'll be, okay?" his mom said.

"I'm a big lad now. I'll be fine," he said, giving them both a long hug.

He wished he'd been on a flight too, but his course in New York to learn more about robotics and forget about losing Rachel was still five weeks away. Hoping to lighten the clouds of despair, Ethan headed into town, hoping to find James. He hadn't heard from him for weeks, which was strange. He could have headed to the cricket club to join the married guys there for a Friday night pint or two, but opted to take a short taxi ride into town.

He spotted Rachel and her buddies, so he tried out the other club, 'The Groove.' He sipped his pint and surveyed his new surroundings. Red and black neon signs lit every outlet, a real throwback to the 80s, but still a tidy place.

Whilst checking out the local talent, a blond hippy looking girl took his eye. On finishing his pint, he headed onto the dance floor, towards her flowing hair and swinging arms. She was totally lost to the music, but he got a reaction when he high fived one of her stray hands. She raised her head to reveal a relaxed, friendly face. Gesturing her apology, she raised her hand and returned a casual smile.

"Ethan," he shouted over the music.

"No, I'm Ruth," she replied with a broad smile, revealing her pearly whites, before re-entering her own world. As the song changed, he realised the music was winning and decided another pint was in order. Both Rachel and James had labelled it as a place for nutters, but all seemed well and the 80s music was a refreshing change.

After returning to the bar, he noticed a stunning beauty strut into the club. Jet black bobbed hair framed her pale complexion, and her athletic look demanded his attention.

After admiring her from afar, she caught his glance and returned a warm smile. It was the prompt he needed, so he casually strolled over and took in her full look. A smooth, tight black skirt and white tailored blouse. She'd got the look of a naughty secretary down to a tee, with bright red lips and nails, with stilettos to match.

"A fan of 80s music, I presume," Ethan said with a confident tone.

"One of my pleasures," she replied with a teasing glint in her eye.

She introduced herself as Jennifer and, far from waiting for Ethan to seduce her; she worked on impressing him. Ethan was eager to listen to someone so stunning and smart. Jennifer worked as a medical researcher, a truly fascinating job. She became more confident, teasing the tip of her tongue on her lips. She was definitely the hunter, which suited Ethan just fine.

Ethan mentioned his love of cricket, but she gave him a quick kiss on his cheek to distract him. Stopping to inhale her sweet alluring scent, a mix of jasmine and orange blossom. He leant in closer and felt her slim lips on his for the first time. He embraced her as their kiss intensified and moved his hands over her firm, toned body.

Her mood suddenly changed. She grabbed his hand and quickly rushed him back to the bar. "Let's get some shots!"

Whilst waiting for the busy dude behind the bar, Ruth appeared next to Ethan. "You seem a nice fella. Do you play sports?" Ruth's nervous patter showed she was not used to approaching guys.

"I play cricket every Sunday morning," Ethan casually responded.

"I love cricket," she fired back. "Can't stand the esports rubbish. It's better to see an actual game."

Glancing across his shoulder, Jennifer had got the attention of the dude and was getting their shots sorted. "I play for the team in Rose Village."

"That's close to me. I might come and have a gander."

"Got a game Sunday, if you fancy it."

The impatient Jennifer dragged her nails firmly across Ethan's bum to regain his attention. She guided his hand to the shot and now she had his attention asked him, "do you want to know my secret?"

"See you Sunday morning, if you make it?" Ruth said, losing his attention to the dark-haired beauty.

Ethan gave a casual reply. "Yeah, I'll be there."

"Hope so," she replied before she returned to the dancefloor.

Ethan turned back to Jennifer, shrugging his shoulders. "Stalker alert." A cheeky smile spread across his lips as he stroked his hand down her side. "So, what's your secret?"

"I like dicks," she said. She leant away to gauge his reaction as she smirked. "They fascinate me."

Ethan re-engaged after her surprising frankness had shaken his confidence. "I have a splendid example," Ethan laughed nervously, but the intense look in Jennifer's mesmerising eyes held firm for a moment before she playfully placed the tip of her finger on her bottom lip and tilted her head to the side. With a cheeky tone, she asked, "Should I take you to my examination room?"

"Only if you wear your lab coat. I'll call a taxi?" Ethan said, with a stirring in his loins.

"No need. We can walk from here. My place is just round the corner."

They downed their shots and headed for the exit. Their walk gathered pace as the excitement overcame them. When they got to her place, which was above the barbers, they stepped through a door to find the base of the stairs. They kissed passionately like new lovers do, and she led him above 'Todd's' into what was a sparsely furnished room. A pair of speakers and a docking station, a locked grey steel cabinet, a desk by the window with a 3D printer sat on it, and a high-quality massage bench in the centre of the room. The dark green leather bench folded up to provide a seat and backrest for its visitor.

"Hope all that cricket hasn't turned you into a bore?" Jennifer teased.

"No, I'm up for most things," he quipped.

"Will you let me play?" she enquired. "I love to play," she added excitedly.

"How can I resist?" he responded with an open-handed gesture, reflecting the air of wonderment about what this energetic beauty had in store for him.

She was almost bouncing on the spot; such was her excitement. "Let me change into my lab coat. I could do a striptease for you."

"Yes please," Ethan replied. He was back in dream territory.

"Okay, no touching though." She stepped behind him and pulled his hands together. A swift Click! Click! Had handcuffed him to the raised bench.

"Cool, this is fun." Ethan enjoyed the surprise introduction of the restraint.

Jennifer popped into her bedroom and returned holding her lab coat and a key.

"What's the key for?" Ethan enquired with just a touch of worry in his voice.

She ignored the question and switched on the music. Cranking up the volume to create the mood for dancing.

Waving her arms in the air like Ruth had done in the Groove held a new significance. She was dancing for him. She danced up to him and stroked his cheeks with her hands before planting a kiss on his forehead.

Ethan took in a deep breath, her sweet scent filling his nostrils as the bulge in his trousers called for attention. She spotted his arousal growing and stroked a delicate nail over his bulge. "Later."

Returning to her dance, she slowly unzipped her skirt to reveal red lace panties. She turned around to the music like a stripping ballerina in a music box. Bent over facing away from him, she slid the skirt over her tight butt; she glanced around to catch him staring and returned a fun smile before she straightened up and turned to face him. Keeping her eyes on him, one button at a time, she undid her blouse from the bottom, revealing her toned stomach. Ethan's pulse was already racing. He shuffled in his seat, trying to release the discomfort of the erection cramped in his shorts.

As she gradually reached the top, she slipped her blouse off and onto the floor to reveal her matching bra framing her petite yet ample breasts.

The music changed, as did her mood. She stopped her gyrations and slipped on the lab coat, whilst fastening the buttons and concealing her beautifully toned body. She firmly proclaimed, "right then, my turn to play."

After the first round of tantalising joy, Ethan was more than ready for round two.

She tilted the bench back and with Ethan lying on his back. Click! another cuff goes on to his ankle and with a sudden panic he moved his other leg away.

"Naughty boy." She playfully slapped his leg.

Jennifer ignored his petulance and undid the buckle of his belt and tantalisingly unzipped his trousers. "Think it's confined in there." She pulled his top up and kissed his navel before returning her attention to his trousers. Ethan lifted his waist as she slipped his trousers to his ankles.

Click!

Now fully tethered, Ethan was not sure if he should partake in such pursuits with a woman he'd known for less than an hour.

Returning to his head, she grabbed his hair and pulled his head back to give him an arousing passionate kiss. Her other hand caressed his chest and moved over his stomach. Breaking away from their kiss, she looked at his excitement growing.

Jennifer stroked his dick with a fascinating interest, seeming for a moment to be lost in thought. She picked up her mobile and scanned his dick. "It is an interesting specimen."

"Thank you." Ethan replied, a proud smile appeared on his lips at the thought of his penis being in a collection. Initially unnerved, Ethan calmed, hoping to enjoy this new experience.

Decisively, Jennifer stepped back into gear, "it's time for some fun." She strode over to her desk and opened a drawer. Ethan lifted his head to see what she was doing.

She lifted out an oversized digital stopwatch, placed it on the desk, and tapped the top to start the timer. She returned to Ethan's side and calmly stated, "don't come too soon or, I will," she paused for effect before her hand delivered a mighty slap across his dick, "chop it off!"

He took a deep breath, trying to conceal the pain. "We'll have no chopping off, thanks," he calmly stated, trying to maintain the fun.

She spoke with an assured strength. "I'm not joking, thirty mins or off it goes," as she was speaking, she took some elastic bands from her lab coat pocket and placed them over his dick, she doubled them over for a tight fit, then tantalisingly rolled them down to the base of his shaft. She ran her tongue up his throbbing shaft and gave a delightful suck to the tip of his dick. She glanced at his beaming smile of appreciation before she nonchalantly turned away.

Taking the key from her pocket, she unlocked the cabinet. It had intrigued Ethan to know what was in there. He'd not experienced the kinkier side of sex and figured it was as good a time as any to start, but when she switched on the light for him to see, his mood of aroused fun changed to panic. The crazy dick enthusiast that had handcuffed him to the bench had a growing collection of dicks.

All colour drained from Ethan's face as the horror appeared before him. The cabinet had a collection of nine flaccid dicks mounted on spikes with a 3D printed erect specimen behind them and, more ominously, one bare spike awaiting her next exhibit. She lifted one short fat shrivelled example and read from the blood-stained wooden base, "twenty-six minutes, twenty-five seconds. He was a nice guy, but he didn't hold on long enough." She looked back at Ethan. "Last thirty mins, give me your seed and you go free. I have a store of them in the fridge." She shrugged. "Well, okay, only one so far."

"What the fuck?" Ethan screeched.

She returned the plaque to the cabinet and returned her attention to his softening cock.

"We don't want you going soft."

"Why?" he asked, not really wanting to know the answer.

With the back of her fingernail, she stroked his testicles. "I will have to open these to find the seed."

He gulped at the thought and hoped for a return to glory; he had an idea.

"Put your breast in my mouth. That'll get me rock hard."

She liked the idea and stepped back into flirty mode, slipping her lab coat off in time to the music. Then she undid her bra to reveal her cute breasts. She leant over him and teased him for a few minutes, with him getting the occasional touch with his outstretched tongue.

"It's working," he said.

She looked to check, and her breast came into range. He got his teeth onto her nipple and bit hard. Jennifer moaned like she was enjoying it and rested her body on him, but the initial pleasurable moan grew into a groan of pain. She tried to pull away.

His grip was firm. He was not letting go.

"And what was your next move?" she stated curiously as she attempted to prise open his jaw.

He spoke through his teeth, "handcuffs off."

"Not a chance," her curt response.

He bit yet harder, and she winced before noticing his cock was now back at its best. She jerked aggressively at it, and he was soon nearing climax. That was until she stuck her nails into his balls. The pain forced him to bite through the rest of her nipple; it was now in his mouth and Jennifer was again free.

"Bastard! Give me my nipple back," she demanded as he was holding it between his teeth.

"The cuffs," he muttered through his teeth.

"Not a chance."

He dropped it into his mouth, swallowed, opened his mouth and proclaimed, "all gone."

She lashed out a stream of punches into his face until she noticed the blood coming from her wound and she stormed off to her bedroom.

Jennifer returned with a temporary dressing over her breast and two devices, the first a small guillotine-like tool for trimming the end of cigars. Ethan's brow creased with confusion for a moment, but his body began frantically wriggling as she was trying to hold him steady to place the device over his nipple. Once in position, she pulled it through. Her eyes met his and a devilish grin appeared on her face, and Ethan's shouting ceased.

Click!

Ethan let out a scream, which she ignored as she peeled back the dressing and placed Ethan's severed nipple over the bleeding hole where her own nipple had perkily stood.

She grabbed the second device, a larger version of the first one. Ethan knew its purpose. He screamed louder and louder and struggled with all his might. She couldn't hold him steady enough, so she climbed onto the bench and sat on his stomach to hold him steadier.

"Got you now," she shouted as she secured the device in position.

Much calmer, she climbed back down and selected the empty plaque she had prepared earlier.

Ethan struggled, screamed and pleaded, but could do nothing to prevent it.

"Twenty-four minutes, forty seconds. You might have made it if you hadn't pissed me off."

Click!

Ethan lifted his head to see blood pulsing out with semen from where his penis had been. His screaming reached another crescendo before the darkness took his screams as he blacked out.

Chapter 13

The clean-up job was easier for Jennifer with Ethan passed out, and her routine was getting rather slick.

One handed, she pulled a thick dressing from the cabinet and slapped it over the open wound on Ethan's groin followed by a four-kilo kettlebell to help stem the bleeding. She didn't want to kill him; she preferred letting death slowly take her victims.

Jennifer held the base of the dick in her hand to hold the blood in place as best she could. The next movement was the tricky part as she grabbed the quick drying glue and squirted it liberally around the spike and the base. It was difficult with one hand, but hiring an assistant for such a deed would require a rather awkward interview. She'd asked her boyfriend Jake to help, but it was no surprise he declined. She'd devised a clamp for the empty plaque to help keep it still whilst she applied the glue. Carefully, she slid the dick down the spike onto the glue and held it in place. She'd become more proficient with each exhibit. The results of her speed had also delivered a penis that largely kept its shape with the help of the spike.

Whilst the glue dried, she thought of her faux par at school, which drove her unhealthy obsession with dicks. Her school life had been fine until her overzealous investigation in a biology lesson. She'd got carried away with dissecting a rat in class and when one guy spotted her severing the rat's penis, word spread quickly around the school she was the cock killer. School life was very different after that, and they believed any stupid rumour. It made her life a living hell, but the upside was an intense focus on her studies, which got her a place at medical college.

With the glue suitably dry, Jennifer pulled out a drawer and lowered the spiked penis into a mix of sodium nitrate and a resin glaze which she used to help preserve her exhibits. She couldn't stop the shrinkage, but the 3D printer kept a physical comparison of the proudest moment of her samples.

She didn't have long before Ethan would come around, so she grabbed the syringe and filled the vial with her mix of Rohypnol and a horse tranquilizer. Pushing his head to the side made the entry point on his neck easy. It would be a couple of days before he came round, if at all.

After she's sewed on Ethan's feeble nipple, she stared in the bathroom mirror, intent it was only a temporary fix. An unwitting volunteer would provide a better replacement.

The dressing over Ethan's gaping wound had stemmed the bleeding. But to finish the job, she needed to fit a catheter and stitch around to close the wound. Fitting the urethral catheter was the poignant part of the process, which always gave her flashbacks to an incident during her medical training.

Jennifer had been enjoying medical training and the blossoming relationship with her lecturer. The lecturer was the first guy to take her seriously. She did everything for him, both at the hospital and in his bedroom, much to the displeasure of her study friend Lucy, who told her to keep a focus on her studies with the catheter fitting assessment due.

Not taking Lucy's advice proved costly. Poorly prepared with only a quick comment from her lecturer brought her world crashing down. "It needs to be inserted firmly. When it's in far enough, you'll know."

She didn't force the tube in far enough and inflated the anchoring balloon inside his urethra. The patient held onto the pain for a short time before he passed out.

"What have you done?" the adjudicator shouted.

Jennifer panicked and ripped the catheter out through his penis. The guy shot bolt upright, letting out a deathly scream holding his dick as blood spurted out. The other students pulled Jennifer away from him with the catheter still in her white knuckled grasp.

The guy sued the hospital, and they kicked her off the programme with her lecturer come lover serving an order for her not to return to the medical profession in any form.

Some would have taken heed that the profession wasn't for them, but she'd spent the whole of her school life and six years at medical college telling everyone, "I'm going to be a doctor."

After twelve months of grieving, she'd contacted the hospital and spoken with the lecturer who'd dropped her emotionally, as quick as he'd kicked her out of the hospital. He had tried to show some of his familiar composure, but when pushed to give her another try, his words cut into her. "Jennifer, you needed more practice, but you panicked and that's unforgivable. I would warn anyone against letting you suck their dick. Let alone anything else. Have you considered working at a mortuary? At least their patients are already dead." He had followed his verbal strip of her decency by laughing down the phone before breaking off the call.

Jennifer took his advice, even though he'd clearly meant it as a joke. She gained work with a funeral director, and her fascination with male genitals continued to grow.

After experimenting on deceased guys when she agreed to stay over at the funeral parlour, she found fitting a catheter without a penis in the way was far easier.

She'd also become more proficient at dealing with her growing penis collection and secured Ethan's member to its plaque in two minutes flat, and she was into more sewing practice to close the gaping hole in his groin.

With Ethan sewn up, she video called the only man she could trust.

"Where were you again?" she asked.

"I had to collect some work from the stonemasons."

"When you hadn't appeared by nine, I played on my own again. Jake, I have a task for you." She moved the phone for him to see the body on the bench.

Jake sighed. "What the hell? Not another one."

"Don't be a naughty boy or you'll be next." She wagged her finger at the phone.

"Seriously, why would I put up with this shit?"

"A pleasant night in the cottage, which may include a blow job?" She said before rolling the tip of her tongue around her lips.

"Okay. As long as there's no biting."

"No biting, I promise." She put her index finger in her mouth and slowly slid it out, with Jake's eyes locked on her.

"You're paying for the train," he said.

"Doing it now. We've got an hour to get to the station."

"I'll be there in ten."

"Love you." Jennifer blew a kiss down the phone before she ended the call.

Jake had been the only successful visitor to her place. He

passed the test, and they'd been dating on and off for the last year, but every time he cancelled a date, she'd head out for her own fun and sometimes he'd get a late-night call.

Jennifer finished tidying up Ethan by covering his groin in silver gaffer tape. She giggled to herself as she did it. If he recovered, getting the tape off would be as painful as the click.

When Jake arrived with the Bass drum flight case, she'd bound a hood to Ethan's head and applied gaffer tape to keep his arms and legs together.

Jennifer couldn't have moved the body, but Jake was a strapping six foot seven and his time in the gym had been well spent. He'd have comfortably carried two guys of Ethan's size.

With tickets printed and the drum case in the back of his SUV, Jennifer grabbed an overnight bag and joined him in the truck. "Did you remember your drumsticks?" she asked.

He held them up. "Nobody takes a drum without sticks."

"Just checking."

The sight of a big bloke carrying a drum case with a pretty lady holding onto his forearm drew attention, but only in the same way, as if he'd been carrying her over his shoulder. Polite smiles greeted them as people either stepped aside or held a door open for them.

Sat facing each other with the Drum case between them, dissuaded people from sitting with them. Not that many people ventured to the North Pennines late on a Friday night.

His other truck was a couple of hundred yards away from the train station. Jennifer skipped ahead and brought the truck to Jake. It was dark, but they headed back up to the previous drop point.

Jake dropped the case off the back of the truck, then jumped down and walked towards the edge of the ditch. He stepped back, burying his nose in his arm. "Wouldn't it be better to just kill and bury them?"

"Got to give them a chance."

"Chance. Tied up and hooded, miles from anywhere in the biting cold. Are you bloody kidding?"

"What do you suggest?" Jennifer asked.

"Take the tape off his arms and legs."

"Okay, if you insist." Jennifer wrapped her arms around her body.

"It won't make any difference," Jake said, as he pulled the tape off Ethan. "He won't get out of this deeper ditch."

Jake pulled the case towards the stench and, holding onto the case strap, he tipped Ethan headfirst into the eight-foot ditch.

No moans or groans followed the crunching thud.

"It's time for your treat." Jennifer turned away and climbed back into the truck.

* * *

"Weren't expecting you," Jennifer's mom said as she opened the door to Jennifer and Jake with the sound of dogs barking.

"Me neither, thought you were away getting some sun, so thought we'd have a couple of days up here, keep an eye on the cottage and the dogs," Jennifer said, as she stepped inside with Jake timidly following.

"We got back yesterday," her mom said.

"Hiya Darling, this is a pleasant surprise," her dad said, as he appeared from the kitchen with a couple of hot drinks. Jennifer stretched up to his cheek and gave her father a polite peck. "We were just going up. I've only just locked the dogs in the back, so best leave them till the morning. Put another couple of logs on and get yourselves a drink."

"Will do."

"I made your bed up after your last visit. Do I need to put the heater on, or will Jake keep you warm?"

"Mom, we'll be fine," Jennifer stroked Jake's back. "You'll keep me warm, won't you?" Jake smiled and pulled her onto his lap. "Night Mom!"

Without a care in the world, Jennifer got the fire going again and settled into a relaxing night with Jake. Her mind slipped back to Ethan and how she'd tempted him away from the other girl who may have treated him better. Who was she kidding? She would've treated him much better. Lashings of red wine took away her shadow of regret and she snuggled into the forever accommodating Jake.

Jake was a guy she could trust. If only he didn't keep working late. Jennifer only misbehaved when she thought he may be with someone else. She needed to work hard to make up for her indiscretion and kept to her word by pleasing him. She teased him with nibbles, but resisted the urge to bite and made all the moaning noises he liked to give him maximum pleasure. The delight was hers too; she loved nothing more than getting her lips around a dick.

With no further thought of Ethan, they headed up to bed and had a peaceful night. Jake awoke with a powerful erection the following morning and Jennifer climbed on. Her mom interrupted their fun when she opened the door to bring in their morning coffees. Jennifer complained she hadn't knocked, but her mom continued in unapologetically and placed their drinks on the bedside cupboard, ignoring her daughter naked astride her lover.

The breakfast table was frantic with the dogs happy to see Jennifer, but the planned sexy time with Jake would not be possible with her mom and the dogs buzzing around. "We're heading back before you get the video camera," she announced with a joke and a smile.

"There's no need. We'll give you space," her dad said.

"It's okay. They have called me in for an extra shift tonight. Can't turn down the cash. We're looking for a house." Jennifer nodded to Jake.

"Splendid news. Really pleased you've clicked so well." Her mom reached across the table and lovingly stroked her hand.

Late morning, Jake and Jennifer said their goodbyes and headed to the train station.

"Can't believe they still think you're a nurse?" Jake said.

"Shut it. I'm never telling them."

Chapter 14

After awakening in the ditch and finding himself sharing it with a dead guy. Ethan knew he needed to get out to survive.

Ethan still had no recollection of how he'd ended up in the ditch and his calls for help were lost in the cold air. The ditch was too deep to climb out and the deceased rotting corpse was evidence that escape was his only chance of survival. Stuck in the ditch, he'd come up with a plan for escape, but it meant Ethan would have to do the most unthinkable, inhumane things. He hoped for further inspiration, but nothing came.

He placed his palms together and bowed his head reverently. "Lord, forgive me for what I must do and give me the strength to survive. Amen."

Ethan leant towards the deceased guy and lifted the dead guy's shirt. His flesh was black and blue, with maggots crawling through holes in his flesh. Ethan retched again and threw up over the guy.

With his nostrils full of the smell of his own sickness and the stench of the deceased, he could hardly take a breath, but each poisoned breath he had to draw made him more determined to free himself of the ditch.

He lifted the guy's hand and pulled; the body moved with his head dropping forward and maggots falling from his eyes.

He'd hoped the arm would pull free, but no such luck. Ethan positioned his foot under the guy's armpit and gave it a sharp tug. This time the arm came free from its socket and Ethan vomited again over the maggot ridden corpse. The overwhelming smell of rotting flesh powered through any hope of recalling anything else. He would only escape the deadly reek if he could get out of the ditch. Using the body of the guy was his only option. Ethan looked up to the skies and attempted to inhale some cleaner air, but the stench won.

Ethan set back to his gruesome task and pulled the other arm from the socket and dropped it onto the other. The legs were next. He lifted the guy's leather boot and read the writing on the side. "Another Six." They were more like size nines, "strange thing to have on a boot."

Placing his foot in the man's groin, he pulled only for the boot to pull free of his foot. Maggots dropped to the ground from the boot, and he threw it down, brushing a maggot from his top. Retching would not help him. He focused on the task, brushed the maggots off the foot, and yanked it. The foot broke away from its ankle, and more maggots spilled from the soggy joint. Ethan bent the leg for more purchase and stamping his foot into the guy's groin to break it free. He attempted to pull it through, but it got stuck in the tapered trouser leg.

He'd hoped he didn't have to, but removing the guy's trousers became the only option. In his woe, he realised perhaps he was the lucky one. He opened the guy's trousers to see the shiny grey tape over his groin matched Ethan's.

Ethan kicked at the sorry guy's hips to free the femur from its socket, and he added it to the pile. The maggots had helped his next task as he easily stripped the flesh from the limbs. Past any further retching from the pungent flesh or his grotesque actions. Ethan only had one thought on his mind.

Survival.

One by one he forced the end of the bone into the wall of dirt, then pushed it across the corner and into the other side, to create a ladder of bones in the corner.

After forcing the last bone into place, Ethan stepped back, pleased with his ingenuity. It was time to rid himself of the maggot infested ditch and its deathly stench. Stepping onto the first bone, it slipped out of the mud wall. He pushed the bone in further and decided speed would be his friend. Each bone moved and slipped out from its home as he stepped higher, but the ledge was in sight and he launched his torso over the edge, but after frantically scrambling at the crumbling edges. It called him to return unceremoniously into the ditch.

The pain in his head exploded again, as did tears of despair.

All cried out. He stood again with renewed vigour and frantically brushed off the maggots, who were looking for more flesh to gorge on. Desperation tortured him as he set about rebuilding his ladder. With it half re-assembled, he screamed out his frustration. "It won't work."

After the pain in his head subsided, he sat to rethink his strategy whilst staring at the half re-built bone ladder. Repositioning the bones on either side of the corner and using a thigh bone as a hammer, he knocked each bone as straight as he could, deep into the mud wall to form grip and step points.

He threw the thigh bone out of the ditch with a renewed confidence he was getting out. The bones held much firmer, and he comfortably stepped from point to point to complete his escape with a roar of relief. He looked back into his temporary prison with a proud smile. "I'm a survivor," he said to the ditch. Despite lacking the evidence of his manhood, or any recollection of his recent past, he was sure he'd never felt more like an alpha male.

He took in the stark surroundings. An unkempt grassy field stretched to the horizon, broken only by small mossy mounds of rock peeking through the ground. The panoramic view held more green hills, with larger rocks scattered around the landscape.

How did he get there?

With the light of the day diminishing, survival was far from secure. With a sodden shirt, damp trousers and shoes more fitting for a boardroom, he needed shelter and protection. He picked up the thigh bone he'd used as a hammer. He held it aloft and stared at it. With nothing else to defend himself, he hoped he wouldn't have to use it.

Chapter 15

Ethan surveyed the area, looking for signs of a solitary cottage, but only rolling hills of green land were around him. The only sign of any life were tyre tracks. That must have been how he'd got dumped in the middle of nowhere and left to die.

Following the faint tyre marks could lead him to a prompt demise, but it provided his only chance of reaching safety.

After an hour, the failing light hid the tyre marks, so Ethan headed further down into the valley. Logic told him there may be a stream to give him relief from the growing pain from each involuntarily dry swallow.

A further hour and the sun had dropped behind the hills. He stopped to rest on a rock, but the wind blew through him, making his teeth chatter. As the night wore on, the chilly breeze would bite deeper, and his chances of surviving the night came into question. He had to keep moving.

The faint sound of water trickling gave him renewed hope. He quickened his pace. More vegetation came into view, which provided some shelter from the wind, but his co-ordination diminished, and he fell face down into a bush of lavender. He lay still, concerned for injury, but the spike of adrenaline warmed him with no undue harm.

Taking a moment to rest in his prostrate state, the piney

scent reminded him of being home with his folks. It brought him a glimmer of hope his memory may return. He pulled himself back to his feet and scrambled through the heather until he reached a narrow stream. He fell to his knees and scooped up the freezing cold water; it revived him and cleared the knifelike stabbing in his throat, but the chill of the water drove deep inside him to make him shudder.

He needed to keep moving, but with only the moonlight to guide him down stream, progress was slow. Something behind him moved in the bushes. Ethan turned sharply, swinging his bone of protection as he growled into the darkness. The rustling of a bush and a wolf like creature fleeing reassured him imminent danger had passed, but it also confirmed it wasn't in his head and something big enough to do him harm was stalking him.

When clouds covered the moon, pitch blackness forced him to stop. He crouched down in a bed of heather beside the stream. He needed rest, but he couldn't settle as the bushes and twigs murmured to him. The shivers returned briefly, but eyes staring at him through a bush spiked his adrenaline and all thoughts of the cold disappeared as surviving the next few minutes took his sole focus.

The creature inched closer. Each time Ethan glanced away from the staring eyes to check around him, closer still, it came. Ethan's chilly hands tightened around the thigh bone. As the creature came closer, he heard another sound behind him. He turned to put his back to the stream and his head snatched back and forth as two sets of eyes were barely a meter away.

Ethan swiped the bone near to the closest on his left and the creature jumped back. The creature on the right leapt towards him, but with a swift backhand, he connected with the head of the creature. It scampered away. The other animal snarled. Ethan snatched his head around, but the other animal didn't return. Relief flooded Ethan like a warm shower when the animal on the left stopped its snarling and bolted away.

"Help! Help!" He shouted into the darkness. He rose to his feet and stumbled out of the bushes. He needed to follow them. If they were wolves, they'd be back in numbers to finish him, but if they were dogs. People were within range. "Help! Help!"

Climbing a bank, Ethan saw a light in the distance. Maybe a mile away, but the small lamp shone like a lighthouse to the seas. Stumbling over rocks, bushes and uneven land, Ethan scampered towards the beacon of hope.

Adrenaline surged through his veins and pushed him towards the small cottage. As he neared safety, the sound of several barking dogs from inside the cottage presented an additional risk. If someone released them, they'd be on him in seconds. He'd just about scared off two, but three would certainly take him down. His pace increased. He needed to get to the door before they were let out.

With a modicum of relief, he reached the solid oak door and slapped his hand against it. The dogs erupted into what seemed like a vicious pack, desperate to kill. "Can you help me?" Ethan shouted with a defeated desperation through the door.

"Easy!" a strong, commanding voice sounded from behind the door. The ferocious pack calmed to excited barks as the bolts slid across the locks at the top of the door. "Back!" The man kicked the bolt at the bottom of the door to release it.

Ethan glanced at the bone fixed into his frozen grip. He wanted to drop it or throw it away, but it had become one with him. Ethan's last sliver of strength left him, his legs gave way, and he collapsed against the door as the enormous man cracked the door open a fraction.

The man stood over Ethan, a crumpled mess on the floor with his white knuckles holding onto his protection.

The man called back into the log cabin, "it's another one."

Chapter 16

How Ethan got into the log cabin, he didn't know.

He awoke to a warm aroma of burning wood. As he slowly raised his head to see the log fire, a middle-aged, curly, dark grey-haired woman shot to her feet. "I'll get you a hot drink."

A heavy thud to his side arrived without warning, sending a wave of pain through him. "How you feeling, fella?"

Ethan looked to see the man's palm resting on the thick blankets covering him. It had been a kind pat, but every part of Ethan ached. "Head's spinning." He retched, but nothing came.

"Misses is getting you a drink. Can you sit up?"

Every bone and every muscle screamed as he forced himself upright. The room was basic, but it was warm. After spending time in the ditch and wandering lost, anywhere would be great but the kind woman passing him a hot chocolate and the guy's face of grave concern re-assured him he'd reached a place of safety to re-energise and collect his thoughts.

"You look confused. Were you drugged?" he asked.

"I guess so. I don't know how I ended up in a ditch. Don't even know who I am."

"It'll come back. I'm sure," the woman said kindly. "I'm

Mary and he's Max. Don't worry. We'll look after you until you're ready to head out again."

Max pointed to Ethan's ankle and shared a glance with his wife. "The catheter is a clue. The last guy had one."

"I'm sure the catheter is new; I've also got gaffer tape over my groin."

"The last guy was the same. It was about twelve months ago. We spotted him shivering when the dogs found him. Thankfully, they didn't attack him. When I brought him in, he was still in shock. He'd had his manhood chopped off and the same catheter fitted."

"Did he find his way home?" Ethan asked.

"Sadly not. He'd been with us for a couple of days and seemed to be okay, but when he didn't respond to come down for breakfast. I found him lying in a pool of blood on the spare bed. He'd slit his wrists. If only he'd waited a day, my daughter's a nurse, she was coming to help him."

Max responded to a worried-looking Ethan. "It's okay, we've got a new mattress. Stay with us till you get your strength back and, hopefully, your memory."

Ethan read the sadness on her face. "He didn't get his memory back, did he?" She averted her gaze to the fire. Ethan turned to the man. The lines on his face said most of it, but a slow shake of his head confirmed it.

"The lad struggled. We thought he'd come to terms with it until his actions told us otherwise."

Ethan stared into the fire, the thought of his memory not returning ran through his mind. He lifted his head. "It's what happens from here that matters."

Mary smiled. Max slapped his hand onto Ethan's shoulder, "that's the spirit."

Ethan winced, and Max lifted his hand. "I'm sore all over."

"Sorry, Fella."

Mary made up the spare bed, and with support, they helped him to bed.

* * *

Ethan woke the following morning with his head empty of thoughts or recollections. The only thing he could recall was hearing the couple say the other guy had committed suicide in the same bed. A warm shower freshened him, but the tape on his groin wouldn't budge without further pain, and he wasn't ready for that. He knew over time it would fall away. For now, he had to endure the second skin. Checking his reflection, he saw an array of blueish yellow bruises over his back, shoulders and ribs. Despite the discomfort, they were the only evidence of the evil hands that had tortured him.

Two days later, sitting at the breakfast table, Ethan still had no recollection of his ordeal, but talking with Mary helped.

"You sound like you may be from the midlands area. Someone there may know you."

"I could easily get lost again in the midlands. City folk aren't as kind as you."

Mary smiled. "I guess you're right. I'm sure your memory will return soon." She placed her hand gently on his. "There's no rush to go anywhere."

"Thanks. I really appreciate what you've done for me."

Ethan's eyes flashed wide open. "Take my picture, send it to a missing person's page. Someone will be looking for me."

"Great idea," she said, trying to sound excited.

Ethan saw through her forced reaction and sighed as he dropped his head into his arms on the table. "You have already, haven't you?"

"We did it as soon as you arrived." She stroked the back of his head. She'd taken his picture and shared it with the missing person's bureau, but she didn't have the heart to tell him nobody had called about his picture. The search for the previous guy had brought no joy, either. He'd taken it badly. They'd figured that was why he'd taken his life. She'd taken Ethan's picture whilst he slept and hadn't discussed it with him. "It's only been a few days. Something will catch. I could give my daughter a call. She could check on your catheter?"

"It's okay, I'm causing you enough trouble already."

* * *

A week later.

Ethan had regained his strength, but not his memory. With no feedback from the missing persons agency, he lost patience with his predicament. After finishing a hearty breakfast. Ethan thanked Mary as usual, before stating, "I won't remember anything by staying here. I need to head to Birmingham."

"It's early yet." She rested her hand on his shoulder. "You can stay as long as you want. I enjoy having you here, besides I called my daughter last night. She can give you a lift to Birmingham after checking you over."

"You've been great, but I need to find a way back to my previous life."

"And that was?" Max said with a playful smile

"Engineer. Yes. I'm an electronics engineer." Ethan's hands

grabbed his own head. "I fix robot vacuum's." He held his arms aloft to thank the heavens. "I fix robot vacuum cleaners," he confidently announced. Tears fell from his face as Mary embraced him.

"Can't be many in the midlands," Max said. He grabbed his mobile and asked, "robot vacuum repairs in the midlands."

Ethan and Mary looked hopefully at Max and his mobile, awaiting its response.

Max's mobile answered. "Here are results for robot vacuum repairs in the midlands."

Max looked up to see their eager faces. He didn't want to knock their confidence, but had to answer their glares. "848 results. It's a lot, but it's a start." Max showed Ethan the screen. "Pictures of each shop front. Have a look through. You may recognize one."

They didn't all have a picture of the shop front, but after two hours, nothing looked familiar. The next option was ringing them. Max printed them off and shared them out.

Ethan still had virtually no memory, but he doubted if anyone from his previous life would have been so selfless as Max and Mary. They heard each other repeating the same lines, "Do you repair robot vacuums?" and "Do you have any employees missing?"

They narrowed the search down to 418, who actually repaired robot vacuums. Quoting data protection laws, few shared if they had employees absent. Some asked why they were calling, but when they said the missing guy was five feet nine with short brown hair. The most common reaction was that they'd seen hundreds of guys who could fit that description.

Primed with the list and feeling more confident, Ethan announced he wanted to head off and didn't want to wait for their daughter.

Chapter 17

Max had bought him a ticket and, along with Mary, they took him to the local train station and stood to watch him off.

Ethan pressed his palm against the vibrating train window as the train pulled out. His eyes fixed on Max and Mary as they waved their goodbyes. His gaze held firm long after the bushes and trees obscured them from his view.

Max and Mary were the only people he knew. They'd been kinder to him than he could comprehend. And he'd chosen to leave the comfort of their home. He repeated Mary's words, "You can stay as long as you want. I enjoy having you here."

"So why didn't you stay?" A delicate woman's voice from the seat in front enquired.

She popped her head around and waited for a response.

Ethan looked agog at her. She was younger than him, perhaps early twenties, studious looking and nosey, or perhaps just friendly.

Without invitation, she sat next to Ethan and with her finger she pushed her round glasses up her nose and put her hands together in her lap. "I'm Ashleigh." She gave him a friendly smile.

Ethan leant away for a second before awkwardly putting his hand out, "Hi."

She placed her delicate hand in his, and Ethan held back from crushing her fingers.

"Don't you have a name?" She prompted, ignoring Ethan shifting nervously in his seat.

"You can call me." He paused, hoping his name would pop into his head, but it didn't. "Fella."

"Pleased to meet you." Her face scrunched. "Fella?" She continued, "where are you heading?"

"Berningham?" His brow creased, unsure if he'd pronounced it correctly.

"Do you mean Birmingham?"

"Yes, that's it, Birmingham." His face lit up like his world had re-connected, but it hadn't.

Ashleigh tilted her head forwards towards him and nodded as she asked, "do you usually have a carer with you?"

To avoid being labelled some kind of nutter, Ethan explained about his memory loss and the polite version of the ditch. When he'd finished telling her she was holding his hand and she looked like she was going to burst into tears. He tried to lighten the mood. "Could be worse. They could've killed me?" He smiled, but Ashleigh rested her head on his shoulder and wiped away a tear for his sorry state.

"Have you contacted the police?" Ashleigh asked. "If you have a criminal record, they could identify you with their facial recognition software."

"If I have a criminal record, the police are the last people I want to go to and If I don't, they won't be able to help me, anyway. I don't know who did this to me?" He lifted her chin and straightened her glasses. "Things are looking up. I've met you."

She wiped her face and shared. "I'm supposed to get off at

Stafford."

"I guess that's not near Birmingham."

She shook her head. "Is someone waiting for you in Birmingham?"

Ethan pulled the papers out of his pocket. "Hopefully, one of these places will be glad to see me."

"I repair robot vacuum cleaners, or I used to." He said as she looked at the papers.

She nodded her appreciation; "You're a smart guy, but you hide it well." She gave him a sympathetic smile. "Did you post a missing person's advert?"

"Mary, the lady that helped me, did. No response yet."

"Social media is pretty good for this kinda stuff. Do you have a social media account?"

"No idea." Ethan held out his hands and shook his head. Had she absorbed anything he'd told her?

She placed her hand on his knee and apologised. After taking his picture, she said, "I work as a junior estate agent. Social media is everything. I have contacts everywhere. Someone who knows you will see this." She posted his picture on all her social media platforms, asking for anybody who recognized him.

"Have you sold many houses?" he politely asked.

"Only two small flats. It was my first big viewing in Laversdale. I was hoping to earn some good commission, but the couple said it was too rural." She shook her head as her annoyance boiled over. "Why didn't they look at where Laversdale was before they arranged a viewing? Stupid people."

"It's the stupid people who make the smart stand out," Ethan said with a smile.

Ashleigh made quite the connection with him and his plight.

He was far smarter than he first appeared and a step above the guys in Stafford who were only interested in adding her to their list of conquests. Despondent with the instant gratification culture, she'd grown lonely in her little bedsit. Maybe he could provide some company and cuddles for a while until his memory returned.

With her station approaching, she held his hand and looked into his eyes. "What are you going to do when you get to Birmingham? You have no money"

"I don't know." Ethan shrugged.

"You'll be wandering the streets homeless. I'm not having that. Come home with me!" she said masterfully. "I guess someone up there wants me to help you."

Ethan looked back into her caring, yet hopeful eyes. "How about if my memory comes back?"

"I'll look after you till it does."

"But I need to get to Birmingham."

"We can go to Birmingham together on Saturday."

The announcement of the train approaching Stafford prompted a decision.

"Okay. I'll come with you."

* * *

Ashleigh was trembling with adrenaline after virtually ordering him to go home with her. The sudden burst of excitement was what she needed in her life. They stopped off on the way to the bedsit and she bought him some clothes, including some full-length PJs to avoid having a naked man in her bed. It was a leap of faith to take a guy she didn't know back to her bedsit.

It was going to be cosy, a double bed, a small kitchenette and a sofa, all in one room, never mind the tiny toilet/shower room.

Ethan hadn't mentioned his lack of manhood and he'd hastily agreed to the clothes without having an awkward fitting to negotiate. The itching from the loosening tape over his groin was driving him crazy, but with Ashleigh not leaving his side. He only sneaked an occasional scratch.

In the bedsit, she spotted him rubbing his groin, and he felt a heat burn in his cheeks.

"No need to blush. You need to relax more." She rubbed his shoulders, which made him more anxious. He hadn't blushed because she'd caught him scratching. It was the awkwardness he sensed was coming when he had to explain why he hadn't revealed the information about his penis. It had been perfectly reasonable to say nothing, but now he was in her home, revealing it, or rather not being able to reveal it, had become an issue he didn't know how to solve.

He'd not gone to her place for sex, but they'd been getting on well and she may have thought it would be the next step after their connection on the train. She wasn't an overly sexual character, but he wanted to keep his distance to avoid an awkward revelation.

She'd not noticed his catheter bag tied to the inside of his calf and whilst he had loose trousers on, it was fine, but he wasn't sure the long pyjamas would be so good at concealing a sensitive subject he'd rather not discuss. Ashleigh had seemed to enjoy his company as the lost guy from a Pennines ditch. Maybe she'd paint him in a different light if he revealed someone had found reason to chop his dick off.

Ashleigh put a film on, and they sat together watching it. She rested her head on his shoulder like she had on the train. In the more relaxed setting, he felt like he was shunning her by not putting his arm around her, but his head was full of questions about what could have caused somebody to remove his penis.

Eventually placing his arm around her, she rested her petite hand on his thigh. He felt a stirring in his loins, as if getting the rumblings of an erection as her finger stroked the inside of his thigh. His spare hand touched his groin to adjust himself, only to be reminded a narrow plastic tube represented all what he used to have between his legs.

Ashleigh glanced up at him several times. She couldn't believe how this guy had landed in her solitary world. She was tingling with anticipation for their first kiss and when it reached the boy gets the girl part of the movie; her eyes called him to kiss her.

Every glance from Ashleigh made Ethan feel more worried. Why did she keep looking at him? He wasn't ready for any sexual contact, not that he'd play much of a part, anyway. He maintained focus on the movie, hoping it would last all night.

The movie credits rolled, and Ethan froze in his seat. If she reached between his legs and couldn't find his tackle, she'd probably scream. He had to tell her. But not yet.

Ashleigh sat forward and placed her hand on his chin, gently gaining his attention. "Do you like me?"

"Yeah. You're a nice girl." Ethan replied like he was trying to avoid getting involved with a mob leader's daughter.

Her chest slumped, and she bowed her head before looking up over her glasses. "Don't you want to kiss me?" She pushed out her bottom lip.

"I don't want to take advantage. You're helping me."

"I've not had a boyfriend before. Well, not a proper boyfriend. You could be my first."

Ethan's heart went out to her. She had taken care of him, given him shelter and even bought him clothes. He owed her everything, but he couldn't deliver what she wanted. "I like you, but I can't give you everything you need."

"Just kiss me."

Ethan leant forward and delivered the most caring, thankful kiss to her slim lips and sat back.

"I've received more intimate kisses from my mother. Is it you don't find me attractive?"

"I do. It's just."

"I just want you to hold me and kiss me."

He could do that. Ethan sat bolt upright. "I'm good with that."

Ashleigh welcomed his lips back to hers, and the heat in their kiss grew. As her body warmed to the sensations awoken by his more fervent kiss, her hands slowly rose up the inside of his thigh.

Ethan placed his hand on Ashleigh's, halting her tantalising ascent up his thigh and taking it to his shoulder. His hand stroked around her slender neck and slowly down her near flat chest, finding a concrete hard nipple. She moaned into his mouth at his touch and followed suit, sliding her hand over the top of his shirt and undoing a button to slip her hand over his chest. Her hand moved more frantically before she broke off their kiss. "Where's your nipple?"

"I only have one." He sat forward. "Let's get some sleep." Ethan glanced around the bedsit. "Do you have some blankets?"

"Only on the bed," she said. "It gets cold at night. I was hoping you'd keep me warm."

"You're very forward for someone who's never had a

119

boyfriend." Ethan said.

"Don't I turn you on?"

"You do, you really do, but I'm not ready."

"I'm sorry. You must think I'm some sex starved crazy woman." She stood and rounded the sofa. "You're still confused, aren't you? Please forgive me."

Ethan followed her around the sofa. "You're kinda cute and I like you. Not for giving me shelter, you're smart, you have a cute smile. Not to mention your huge nipples." Ethan laughed for the first time he could remember. Ashleigh laughed too, flicking her own nipples, which made Ethan laugh all the more. They embraced and kissed again. "No sex." Ethan said.

"Just cuddles and kisses," she replied.

"Okay. Cuddles and kisses." Ethan kissed her again, before asking for directions to the bathroom.

Ethan emptied his catheter before he turned to stare at his reflection in the mirror. "She screamed when she found I'd got a nipple missing. What's she going to do when she finds out the rest?"

Chapter 18

"Are you okay in there?" Ashleigh asked through the door. "I need the toilet."

Ethan had changed into the PJs she'd bought, but was nervous about coming out. Clothes in hand, he opened the door to let Ashleigh in as he slipped past her. He grabbed the opportunity to claim the far side of the bed and slipped under the covers.

Whilst Ethan had been in the bathroom, Ashleigh had changed into some cute nightwear, which she hid under a cosy dressing gown. A previous boyfriend had bought her the lace trimmed heart print PJ top and short set hoping to see her wear it, but she dumped him before he had the chance. She'd been saving it for a special occasion, but after six months of no love interest, tonight was her first opportunity. Checking herself in the mirror, her confidence lifted before she sprayed on some of her favourite soft floral scent and stepped out of the bathroom without her dressing gown for Ethan to enjoy the view.

Her big reveal fell flat as Ethan was facing away from her, pretending to be asleep. "You can't be asleep already," she said to the back of his head.

"Not quite," Ethan mumbled in response, without turning

his head.

Ashleigh nearly burst into tears. Perhaps she should have let her ex-boyfriend see his gift in all its finery. Ethan didn't seem to care. She slipped into bed with her back facing him. "Good night."

If that had been her last action of the night, all would have been perfect for Ethan, but after a couple of minutes, she turned over and shuffled a little closer. He could feel her breath on the back of his neck and jumped when she touched his shoulder.

"I thought I'd be the nervous one with a strange man in my bed."

Ethan rolled onto his back. He didn't want to be impolite to the girl who'd shown him such friendship in his time of need. "Sorry. I was thinking back to the ditch. I still don't know how I ended up there."

"It's okay. You're safe now." Ashleigh rested her head on his shoulder and lay her arm over his chest. "I'll look after you till you get your head together." Ashleigh didn't need a fella, hence why she ditched the last guy, but it was nice snuggling up to him. His memory would likely return in a few days, and he'd be off, but she was going to enjoy having him around. He was the best bed warmer that she'd ever had, and he was kinda cute.

Ethan repeated in his head, please don't put your leg over mine, hoping it would work, but slowly her toes crossed his ankle. He moved his foot, but gradually her foot followed. His right leg holding the catheter bag was getting further and further across the bed until it got a glimpse of the chill outside of the covers.

Her knee crossed over his.

Ashleigh hoped he didn't think she was throwing herself at

him, but he was as warm as toast. She inhaled his musky scent. Her heart filled with relief when he put his arm around her and kissed the top of her head. She lifted her head, and their lips met for a lingering kiss.

Despite the secret he was hiding, Ethan took comfort in having Ashleigh close to him. After hugging her, she'd responded with a kiss and he had a sensation between his legs. Sadly, the sensation was the only reaction possible without an erection, which he would've gladly welcomed. Would this be a good time to tell her?

Ashleigh tingled with anticipation, wanting more despite the agreed cuddling and kissing agreement. She slid her knee up his thigh, looking for a sign of his arousal, but Ethan's hand put a polite stop to its progress. She stretched out her leg to find his other leg was almost completely off the bed. Was she scaring him? She was about to retrace when her toes connected with something under his pant leg. "What's that?" she asked politely.

Busted.

Ethan rolled Ashleigh off his chest and propped himself up with an elbow and realised honesty was the right course to follow. "I've got a catheter fitted."

"Did you have a medical problem?" she asked, stroking his chest with the back of her fingers.

Ethan rolled his eyes. "Sort of. When I woke in the ditch, I had no penis and instead this tube ran down my leg to a bag attached to my ankle."

Rather than screaming, she was inquisitive. Ashleigh lifted the covers. "Will you show me?"

She wasn't mocking him; she was genuinely interested in what had happened to him. Who is this girl? She's not freaked out by any of this. Ethan lifted his knee and pulled up his pant leg to reveal the thin tube going into the bag.

"Not that end. The other end." She shook her head and smirked, pointing to his groin. She stretched up and switched on her reading lamp.

"There's not much to see." The joke he attempted didn't receive the slightest smirk. He pulled his PJ's down to reveal his gaffer taped groin and the protruding thin tube.

"I haven't seen many, but it's the longest I've seen." She smiled, gauging his reaction. He saw the funny side and didn't take offence. She prodded around the tube. "Are you sure it's not behind all that tape?"

"I'm sure." Ethan nodded.

"How about there?" She prodded below the tube.

Ethan winced, and his eyes watered as she'd inadvertently poked one of his testicles. He quickly pushed her hand away. "That's my balls."

She put her hand over her mouth, appalled by what she'd done, whilst also holding in a giggle. As he calmed, she asked, "Why don't you take the tape off? See what's going on down there."

"I don't know if I want to. Ripping pubes off my testicles is not on my to-do list."

Ashleigh peered back into the problem. "Some of it is coming away already." With a finger and thump, she grabbed a free edge and gave it a tug.

"Ow!" He yelled. "I've had enough agony for tonight. Shall we look at it tomorrow?"

"If you insist," Ashleigh said, gently tapping the gaffer tape.

Ashleigh pulled the covers back over them and gave a loving moan of pleasure as he pulled her close again. She rested her arm across him to enjoy the calming rise and fall of his chest. His breathing lengthened. Perhaps having shown her his deepest secret had been a release.

Ashleigh wasn't ready for sleep. Her mind was whirring. What had this fella done to warrant someone chopping his dick off? Was he an innocent victim? Don't be stupid. He'd done something serious. Was all this memory loss stuff, bullshit? After about an hour of mentally torturing herself, she figured he'd not shown any signs of harming her. The only harming that was likely would be when she had the twisted pleasure of removing the gaffer tape in the morning. It gave her peace and helped her to sleep.

The reveal had gone better than Ethan could have hoped. She'd shown genuine compassion for his plight and hugged him the same. A smile came to his lips as he relaxed with her arm across his chest. After he'd had his memory wiped, this was a fresh memory to treasure. Hopefully, he could get some sleep without the thought of her having a screaming fit in the middle of the night. Ashleigh's breathing had become steady, and it was time to drift off and pray for some memory to return with the morning.

Chapter 19

Ethan awoke to the smell of breakfast sizzling away. "Bacon, lovely." It sparked a memory. Someone had made him a bacon sarnie. It was a blond woman. He remembered her slapping his face and then he had a flashback of her face being pummelled and a huge guy running towards him.

"Are you okay?" Ashleigh asked with a frown of concern.

"I had a flashback." Ethan said slowly.

"What was it about?" Ashleigh asked.

"Not much, just someone handing me a bacon sarnie." It wasn't something Ethan wanted to share. "Nice PJs, quite the cutie, aren't you?"

"They were a gift from my ex." she casually slipped out. "Given the desperate attempt at a subject change. I would guess it was more than just a sarnie," Ashleigh said.

"I thought you said you'd not had a boyfriend," Ethan said teasingly, with a tilting of his head and a stroke of his chin.

"Get a grip, I'm twenty-three. I've not had a serious boyfriend, though."

Ethan climbed out of bed and gave Ashleigh a hug from behind and a kiss to her earlobe before she shrugged him off to return to the bacon. "If I thought the memory was significant, I'd have said. I think I was in my apartment."

"That is significant. It tells us you have one. Is it above a shop?"

Ethan had a moment of clarity. "Yes, it's above a butcher." He flung his arms around her and lifted her up, to which she let out a scream.

"Put me down, the bacon's ready."

After enjoying a bacon sarnie with some brown sauce. Ashleigh grabbed the plates. "And next. Time to get you in the shower, get you toasty and ready to lose your gaffer tape pants."

"Why the shower?"

"It stinks and more importantly, it's a great waxing tip. It'll hurt less when I pull it off."

"When you pull it off?" Ethan said.

"Yep. I'm coming in with you," Ashleigh said, and a huge grin appeared on her face.

Ethan put his hands on his hips, ready to object, then figured that Ashleigh naked in there with him would be the distraction he needed.

Ethan turned on the shower, and while it was getting hot, he stripped off his PJs. He was about to step in when Ashleigh came in, but he held off to take in the view of her slipping out of her pink PJ set. In any other situation, he would have made love to her right there as she revealed her slim figure.

"In you get. Stop staring." Ashleigh ushered him into the shower like putting a horse into a starting gate before she squeezed in next to him.

Ethan's elbows banged the sides of the shower as he lathered Ashleigh's shoulders before she leant against him, and his hands held her in a soapy cuddle. When she turned to kiss him, tingles ran through his body as they kissed under the showerhead.

Ashleigh didn't want him to regain his memory. She wanted to keep him for herself. Despite the feeling in her core, she didn't need a guy with a dick, she just needed someone to hold her. Deep down, she knew she only had limited time with him.

Suitably warm, she lathered his waist, sending soap through the small gap between his waist and the chastity tape. Pinned into a corner of the shower, he had no complaints when she kneeled at his feet. The first gentle tug brought a controlled moan of discomfort. "I've got an idea." She squeezed out of the shower and quickly returned with nail scissors. "It's okay not going to chop anything else off. I can cut some of the tape away and trim the hair away from the tape." She gave his stomach a soaked kiss to reassure him she was doing it with care.

Trapped in the shower cubicle whilst Ashleigh pulled and cut the tape away, Ethan was both enjoying the attention and equally scared at what she would reveal. He desperately hoped his dick would still be there, but with each cut, he looked down to see the picture he expected. Thick black stitches where his penis should have been. After her error the previous night, she took extra care of his testicles, but she was right; the heat of the shower made the job easier.

"All done," she announced. He helped her to her feet, and they shared another long kiss.

After drying off. Ethan's groin was tender, but she gave him some cream and told him, "Rose and Lavender are far better than the stink from last night."

* * *

Ashleigh's media blast reached two people that Ethan knew.

Rachel stared at her phone for a minute. "Bloody cheating pisshead. Drank so much he doesn't even know who he is. He can fuck off if he thinks I'm going to help him." She threw her phone onto her bed. Although the girl he'd supposedly cheated with, Emma had told her that nothing had happened. Rachel remained incensed by the fact he'd spent time with her.

She'd awoken with a splitting headache. The previous day she'd showed a young couple the house she'd planned to share with Ethan. The similarity to her life plan hit her hard when they mentioned they planned to start a family and agreed to buy the house. Rather than celebrating, Rachel went home and sobbed with a bottle of red. Despite having regrets about how things had ended with Ethan, it wasn't the day to forgive him.

* * *

Unmoved by their evil act. Jennifer and Jake carried on with their lives and were taking the next step in their relationship. She'd not been keen initially, but the mention of starting a family had taken her to a better place and after agreeing to buy a house together, she pledged to Jake she'd put an end to her crazy antics.

They'd just signed for the house and had taken their seats at Robolicious for a celebratory lunch. Whilst waiting for their steaks to arrive, Jennifer sipped some wine whilst she checked the updates on her mobile. Ethan's face scrolled into view on her phone and her perfect day slapped her in the face. "What the fuck? You idiot." She kicked Jake with her stilettoed shoe and punched his chest.

"Hey! Hey!" Jake raised his hands in defence.

"You said give him a chance and now look what you've done."

Jake went cold when he saw Ethan's face. He snatched the phone from Jennifer and read the message. "This guy has lost his memory. If you recognize him. Call me."

"Looks like we've got one more body to sort out," Jennifer said.

"The guy's lost his memory. He's not blabbing on us." Jake shrugged and passed the phone back to Jennifer, shaking his head before putting his pint back to his lips.

Jennifer tapped furiously into her phone, checking Ashleigh's social media profile and her recent comments. Her previous entry before the missing person's post had been a picture with her boss. She worked for an estate agent in Stafford and had closed out her first sale. She was very slight and would not pose any issues if they turned up for Ethan. "Think we need to pay Stafford a visit."

Jake shook his head as Jennifer was making a call. "Hiya, sorry to bother you. I have several buyers looking to move to Stafford. Is your house for sale?"

"Don't think you'd want this place. It's only a small bedsit," the polite voice replied.

"Is it near the high street?"

"Not far. About a mile. Ragland street."

"That might be okay."

Ethan waved his hands in front of Ashleigh's face. "Don't tell them anything."

His frantic attention unsettled Ashleigh, and she gave a rushed reply. "I'm not interested in selling, but I have a two-bed semi-detached for sale opposite. Have a look at our website, Stafford Properties.co.uk. I'm back at work on

Monday. Call me there and we can arrange a viewing."

"Will do. Thanks for the help," Jennifer replied.

"My pleasure."

Ashleigh looked at Ethan like he'd gone crazy. "People looking for houses in Stafford, that's all. It may get me another sale or two."

Ethan let out a heavy sigh. "Guess you're right. Just got to know who you're talking to. Did they give a name?"

Ashleigh shrugged. "No. Don't think she did. Sounded nice enough, though." She frowned. "Are you hiding from somebody?"

Ethan held his palms face up, shaking his head. "I don't think so, but I don't know."

She folded her arms like a worried mother taking a deep breath before letting out a heavy sigh. "I never thought helping you could put me in danger." Conflicted, she slowly shook her head. She didn't want to spoil the connection growing between them, but she hadn't fully considered the risk of taking in a stranger.

Ethan held out his hands. "Nothing has changed from when we met on the train. You know me now. You don't feel threatened by me, do you?"

"I don't. It's just. What if someone's coming after you?" Her eyes filled with worry.

Ethan put his arms around her. "We don't know that?" She rested her face on his chest. "You just shouldn't tell people where you live, that's all." He lifted her chin with his finger and took in her scared eyes before he tasted her salty kiss. The connection he shared with Ashleigh gave him strength, but the thought of bringing her harm bit into his resolve. If someone had left him for dead in a ditch, flashing an "I'm alive" message on social media was not the best idea.

He was sure his memory was returning, but needlessly moving on may put him back. Ethan had quickly grown fond of Ashleigh and wanted to stay with her. Besides, there was no obvious reason to move on without knowing where he lived. Was he being paranoid? It could have been an innocent call. He wanted to check. "Can I call her back to check out the house hunt story?" Ashleigh passed him her mobile, but the number had been withheld.

Chapter 20

After a fruitless trip into Birmingham with no memory triggers, Ethan and Ashleigh enjoyed a relaxing Sunday. They'd popped to the local pub for a carvery, picked up a bottle of red on the way back and were dozing in front of the cricket.

Ethan sat up with a spark. "I play cricket."

"That's excellent. Glad watching this for two hours has not been a complete waste of time." The wine had done its job on Ashleigh and removed her inhibitions.

"Sorry, Ash." The game was pretty much over, so he flicked through the channels and selected a romantic comedy.

"Better," she said as she rested her cheek back on his shoulder.

After the film, the influence of the romance spread to the sofa, and they had their own cuddles.

* * *

Ashleigh looked a cut above in her power suit as she headed out to work. Her transformation wowed Ethan. The petite girl who'd invited him into her bed was again the confident high heeled go getter. "Your challenge for the day. See if you can get the toaster working." She dropped it into his lap and gave him a peck on his cheek.

Ethan sat in the bedsit watching TV with the broken toaster in his hands. After a couple of hours, the challenge of the toaster sparked him into action, and he took it apart. It took him five minutes, and he turned his attention to the papers Max and Mary had printed. Using Ashleigh's laptop, he virtually walked around the vicinity of the repair centres. They all looked familiar, but didn't every town. He deduced he must be from a town rather than a city environment and in the process crossed off more than a hundred entries to reduce his list to 308, with 45 starred as having staff missing. If he called them, it might narrow his search further or even find out where he worked.

Ethan had video called twenty-three of the starred entries but had no luck. He was about to call the next on the list, Baileys Electronics, when a tap came on the door of the flat. He nearly jumped out of his skin. Cold sweats shook him into action. He scrambled to his feet and grabbed a knife from the drawer. A key rattled in the lock before a shoulder nudged the door. Ethan was sure he'd be facing another ditch when the door flung open.

She stood tall and stared at him as he cowered behind the sofa with a table knife. "Fine guardian, you are. What are you going to do with the knife? Spread butter over me."

He stood with a cheesy smile. "Chocolate spread would be better."

"Like the sound of that. Do you want to pop out and get some?" Ashleigh took some money from her purse. "The woman you were worried about has come through, not a psycho after all. She's on the way from Birmingham with her partner to look at the two properties over the road."

"That's splendid news." Ethan said. "For you and me. No nutter chasing after me and you get some more sales."

"And my chocolate treat tonight." She smiled.

Ethan felt a stirring in his loins. It was an itch he couldn't scratch, but licking chocolate off Ashleigh would be a great consolation prize.

Ashleigh spotted his pile of papers. "Any luck with the search?"

"I've narrowed it down. I'm just video calling the ones who said they had missing staff. The connection's not great, though."

"You can borrow my personal mobile. My work phone will be fine for this afternoon."

Taking her phone, he held onto her hand. "You've been so good to me. I don't know if I even want to find my previous life."

"If you get your memory back, it doesn't mean we're through. I enjoy having you around. By the way, could you have a look at this sticking door?"

"Anything for you."

"Don't forget the chocolate." She blew him a kiss and headed off to prepare for her first viewing of the afternoon.

Ethan got straight to fixing the door. He tightened a loose hinge to solve the problem. With her spare key, he checked it a few times before heading to the local shop. He enjoyed being outside and extended his walk to take in a small park and watch kids feeding the ducks. "I could get used to being around here." His pleasurable afternoon lost its edge with the realisation that having his own family wouldn't be possible. He picked up his bag with two tubs of chocolate spread and headed back to the bedsit.

135

Two hundred yards away, he spotted Ashleigh leading the couple to the house opposite theirs. The smartly dressed woman had jet black curls and a pale complexion. She was mesmerising even from that distance. The guy she was with was some kind of bald-headed giant, packed full of muscle. He glanced around before following Ashleigh and the woman through the door.

Ethan felt a chill run through him. Something just wasn't right. Was Ashleigh in danger or was this what truly caring for someone was like, to live in fear of anything bad happening to them. The huge guy didn't look like he was an estate agent. He looked more like a terminator who could rip her apart. A memory returned, which freaked him out. He'd reminded him of the guy who killed the blond in the park, but he was much larger.

Ethan had to do something, but he couldn't confront them. The giant would crush him like an ant. He pulled out Ashleigh's phone and called the police. "I've just spotted the guy responsible for the attack on the blond girl in the country gardens from a few weeks ago."

"You've come through to Stafford Police station. Which country gardens?"

"He's here on Ragland Street. He's just entered a property. A woman is in danger. Please come quickly."

"Could I have your name, please?"

"No. I don't know my name. I've lost my memory."

"But you remember someone from weeks ago." The sarcastic response. "Wasting police time is a serious offence. Which country gardens are you referring to?"

"Near Birmingham. I'm not sure which town."

"You're not helping much." The annoyance growing in her

response.

Ethan's memory returned. "Rose Village. It's near Rose Village."

"I'll pass the details onto Birmingham. I have your phone registered as Ashleigh. Is that your name?"

"I'm not Ashleigh. It's not my phone."

"Sir, can you put Ashleigh on the phone?"

"No. I can't. It's Ashleigh that's in danger."

"Sir. What have you done with Ashleigh?"

"I've not done anything to her. You need to come quickly."

"Sir, I need you to tell me what you've done to Ashleigh."

In his frustration, Ethan ended the call. "Fat lot of good."

Ethan approached the house. The door was open; he wanted to go inside and confront them, but fear held him back.

With a courage he didn't know he had, he peeked through the door.

* * *

Ashleigh had flirted with a few relationships, but the fella she'd met on the train made her feel alive. Apparently matching first names is a good omen for a happy partnership, so she hoped his name began with an 'A' for Andy, Adam, or perhaps Alex. She couldn't call him 'Fella' forever. She thought about him fixing her door and getting the chocolate spread ready.

Tonight was going to be a special night. They were not a perfect couple, but neither were Jennifer and Jake. Jennifer was a confident, attractive woman. Her partner Jake was less so, but he fit the bill as her protector.

Ashleigh kept her smile going as she extolled the virtues of the property and its location. "It's a small, friendly estate. Got locks on the windows, though, just in case." She unlocked the window to get some much-needed fresh air into the room as she pointed out the shared walled garden, but she knew it was a waste of time. She'd initially ignored it when Jake had to turn sideways and duck through each doorway, but it became too obvious a problem. "The location is excellent for access to town, but with the size of Jake, you'd be better off with an older house. The doors will be taller and wider."

"Can we have a look at your place?" Jennifer politely asked.

Ashleigh frowned. "Mine is smaller than this." She shook her head at why they still seemed interested in her bedsit.

"What number is it?" Jake asked.

A chill ran through Ashleigh. They were after her fella. "I'm not telling you where I live." Usually, when a guy of his intimidating size asked her something, defiance was not one of her top five responses.

No sooner were the words out of her mouth, Jake pinned her throat to the wall. "Where's Ethan?"

Ashleigh gasped for air, her body stiff with fear.

Jennifer screamed out, "Where's Ethan?"

The grip on her throat eased enough for her to respond. "I don't know what you're talking about." His choking grip on her throat resumed.

She held up her phone and showed her Ethan's face. "Does this look familiar?"

Ashleigh attempted to feign indifference, but the fear in her eyes burned bright.

"It's time to talk." Jennifer ripped open Ashleigh's blouse to reveal the biggest nipples she'd ever seen on the smallest of breasts. "Hope you weren't fond of those nice nipples."

Ashleigh let out a muffled scream and kicked out at Jake. He didn't take kindly to her dragging a heel down his thigh. He threw her to the floor. She hoped to reach the door as she tried to scramble away, but Jennifer slammed the door shut and Jake pushed her back onto the floor. He sat on her legs and after she failed to wriggle from his grasp; he pinned her hands together over her head. His other hand muffled her scream as Jennifer kneeled at her side.

"One more chance. The guy who lost his memory. Is he at your house?"

The ogre moved his hand for her to speak. She let out a quick scream before his huge hand covered her mouth again. "She's not learning."

Jennifer reached into her jacket pocket and pulled out the cigar clipper. Ashleigh's muffled scream stopped, confused by what she was holding, but her screams piqued again. As much as she struggled, she could not stop Jennifer from placing the clipper over her nipple. Her finger and thumb pulled her nipple through the gap in the device. "Last chance!"

Ashleigh quickly filled her lungs when the hand gave her chance. "Don't," she cried. "34. It's number 34."

"Thank you. Still need a good one of these to replace what Ethan took from me."

Click!

Jennifer slipped the severed nipple into a plastic bag. She dropped it in her pocket and pulled out a small blade. "Not leaving this one to chance," Jennifer said as she jabbed the blade once, twice, three times into Ashleigh's side. Ashleigh took a sharp intake of breath but a hefty strike to the side of her head left her still as they left her bleeding out.

* * *

Ethan had slipped into the house but having learnt his name from the most unlikely of sources he froze with fear, hearing the muffled screams from the other side of the door had stopped him from returning to his previous hell as all the memories of his own demise became clear. He recognized her voice. It was Jennifer. As the handle of the door dropped, he shot into the bathroom.

Jake strode down the stairs with Jennifer close behind as they charged out of the house.

A chill ripped through Ethan as he stepped in to find Ashleigh out cold on the floor with blood seeping through her blouse and pouring her life away onto the wooden floor. His heart turned to iron and pulled him to the floor aside her. The blood seeping from her severed nipple pulled out the memory of his own loss, but his new love for Ashleigh was far deeper and it had realised his darkest fear of bringing her trouble. His head dropped to hers. He dwelt in her grief for a moment before she stirred with a weak moan.

He snatched a handkerchief from his pocket and pressed it to her bloodied side. With his free hand, he put the phone down on her stomach and called for emergency services. "Woman, bleeding heavily, Ragland Street, No. 12 upstairs."

"On our way. Are you with her?"

"Yes, but I need to go." He sobbed.

"Just need you to stay with her and keep pressure on the wound. A paramedic will be with you in six minutes."

Ethan sat up and looked out of the window to see Jennifer looking back out of Ashleigh's bedsit. "I don't have six minutes.

The curly black-haired woman and her bald giant are going to be back before then."

"We've dispatched a unit to the scene, but a community officer will be with you in a couple of minutes. Stay with her and you'll save her life."

The giant reappeared from the bedsit and Jennifer pointed back to where Ethan was holding Ashleigh's life by a thread. "Ashleigh. I'm not leaving you. We can die together."

Ashleigh's eyes cracked open as she coughed back into consciousness. She slowly shook her head and uttered a single word, "run." Her eyes opened wide and stared at him before they slowly rolled upwards as life left her. The world went quiet and still for Ethan for what seemed like an hour, but Jake bustling through the front door, must have only been a few seconds later. Ethan's desire to live returned, but with him already in the house, his escape was blocked. The open window was his only escape. He opened it wider and squeezed into the frame as Jake burst through the door. They both froze for a second as their eyes locked.

Chapter 21

Ethan dropped onto the conservatory roof and jumped down into the walled garden. A gate at the back of the garden provided an exit point. Ethan sprinted through the gate into a small wooded area leading to another housing estate. Not making the mistake of looking around and risking a fall, Ethan focused on controlling his breathing and maintaining his pace.

Not hearing anything behind him, he looked back and there was no sign of the giant on his trail. Ethan had figured as much; the guy was too big to get through the window and with such bulk was unlikely to keep pace with him. Ethan held steady for a moment and regained his breath, whilst keeping a keen eye around him.

His pace had calmed when he stepped through a gulley into the housing estate. It was a mistake. The monster of a man stepped out of a car. "Time to stop running, Ethan." The man called out, but Ethan had no intention of stopping and ran scared back through the woodland. This time he stopped at the midpoint and considered if the car would drive around to catch him on the other side as there was no sign he was being followed.

Ethan ran along the well-trodden route, but with him tiring, to return to the wrong point would condemn him. He made his way along the length of the area, stepping carefully through a denser, overgrown route. Every few steps he stopped and listened, checking he wasn't being hunted. Returning close to the housing estate but some 200 yards from the gulley, he spotted a gate to someone's garden. He tried to peek through to check for a dog. All he needed now was a dog attacking him or, worst still, barking to alert his position.

The old man in the garden nearly had a heart attack when he looked up from tending his flowers to see Ethan's scared face and his finger over his lips, his other hand giving him a palm down, calming action. "I mean you no harm," he whispered.

"Leave my garden at once!" the white-haired, frail man said.

"Sir, I can't do that." Ethan whispered. His hands made a praying steeple on his chin. "Raising your voice again could put us both at risk."

The white-haired man calmed. "Why are you in my garden?"

"I've just witnessed a viscous attack and they're looking for me."

"Don't involve me. I'm eighty-four."

"I don't intend to. Can we go inside?"

"I've not finished here yet. Pass me the lily."

Ethan picked up the small plant like he was partaking in a neighbourhood help program, but the faint sound of an ambulance called the image of Ashleigh lying in a pool of her blood. His heart ached. She'd befriended him, took him in, given him hope, even loved him. She'd have still been alive if she hadn't taken him in.

"And that one." The man's simple request cut through the pain. Ethan pledged silently to avenge their deeds, both for himself and for Ashleigh.

Once inside the house, Ethan peered out through a bedroom

window. The huge guy looked over the fence of the garden three doors away. In the frail man's garden, a kneeling pad, mini fork, and the empty potting tray lay unattended.

Ethan kept his head down as he looked out the front window and saw Jennifer. She was also three doors down, talking at the door with someone and showing them a picture on her phone.

"What are you doing upstairs?" The elderly gent asked from the bottom of the stairs.

"What's the best way to the train station from here?" Ethan asked as he descended the stairs.

"It's quite a way. I could take you in my car," the man said. He rolled his eyes. "If it gets you out of my house."

"Just point me in the right direction," Ethan said.

"Through the woodland and turn left. It's a long walk, though. I don't mind taking you in the car."

With Jennifer close to knocking on the old man's door and the giant of a man covering the back.

Ethan had only two options.

Rely on an 84-year-old man to hold under questioning or make a run for it past the woman and through the woodland before big foot could clamber back to the path. He had a third option. He could stop the man from opening his door, but he'd stressed the old gent enough.

Looking through the front window, the next-door neighbour had just opened the door. Ethan casually opened the door and walked to the pavement. He tried not to look, but felt eyes burning on the side of his head. He couldn't resist turning towards the neighbour and Jennifer. The little old lady pointed to Ethan and Jennifer shouted, "Jake."

She took flight after Ethan, who had ten yards on her and with her high heels; she had no chance of catching him. Not knowing where Jake could be, he avoided the woodland route and stuck to the pavement as it began circling to the left. It continued round and Ethan figured he'd be heading straight back into trouble, but with Jake in pursuit, he couldn't stop running.

The frail man had closed the door behind Ethan just in time, as Jennifer approached. He ignored her knock. She tapped on the bay window, staring at him through the glass. "Are you harmed? That man is extremely dangerous. You're lucky he didn't kill you."

The man came to the window. "I'm a little shook up. It's a lot to take. I'm eighty-four."

"Do you know where he is heading?" Jennifer asked, like the most caring woman in the world.

"He wanted to go to the train station. I offered to..."

"Thanks." Jennifer waved a casual hand and headed back to her car, making a call.

Another gulley came into view, and Ethan took it. The narrow pathway was long and straight. He didn't know where it would take him. Panic filled him as he was approaching what appeared to be a dead end. "If he's followed me into here, I'm stuffed." Ethan's chest ached. Not used to the running and full of stress, he slowed to a walk. As he neared his stop point, to his relief, a ninety-degree turn became apparent.

A voice from behind him at the entrance to the gulley cut his moment of relief short.

"You're a dead man," Jake bellowed as he entered the gulley.

As Ethan took the corner, adrenaline kicked him back into a run towards a main road.

* * *

The exhausted Jake stopped when his mobile rang. "He's heading to the station," Jennifer said.

Jake breathed heavily into the phone. "He's like a bloody greyhound."

Jennifer picked Jake up and drove to the train station. "He'll appear here at some point. If you wait inside, he'll not see you."

"What if he's not going to the station?"

"The old man said he was. If he doesn't appear, we can shake the old man till he squeals."

"Another body to hide," Jake replied with a sarcastic shake of his head.

"If you'd left Ethan tied up, we wouldn't have this mess." Jennifer pushed Jake, encouraging him to get out the car and head into the station. "If I see Ethan outside the station, I'll call you."

Jake loitered just inside the station, munching on an energy bar, ready to nab the unsuspecting Ethan.

* * *

After giving the slip to the muscle-bound freak, Ethan headed back to find Ashleigh. He couldn't leave Stafford without checking on the girl that had helped him.

Two police cars were at the scene with an ambulance.

A police officer stood outside the house and had called to another. The police officer was holding the bag Ethan had used to do his shopping and, with blue inspection gloves, he held a tub of chocolate spread.

Ethan's tears flowed at the thought of the scene they

should've had. He would have spread the chocolate over Ashleigh, and she'd have giggled to his touch as he licked her clean. He could taste the mix of chocolate and her soft skin on his tongue. Kissing her navel and lapping at the chocolate. He would have spread more around those wonderful-. Ethan heaved as her body, covered in blood, returned to his thoughts. Her perfect nipple replaced with a pool of blood on her chest, her white blouse soaked in her blood. He fell to his knees in the middle of the road and threw up.

He looked up when he saw two shiny black boots in front of him. "Not a great idea recovering from your stupor in the middle of the road."

Ethan wanted to tell the officer everything, from his first meeting with Jennifer to the ditch and now Ashleigh. He rose to his feet and her kind hand guided him back to the pavement. Would the officer believe him if he told her? Or would she be like the woman who answered his call?

His prints were all over her bedsit, on the tubs of chocolate spread, and he probably had speckles of blood on his trousers from kneeling by her side. He had no proof Jennifer and Jake had even been there. Speaking up would be the end of his chance to avenge their deeds. He acted drunk to go with the officer's first thought. He staggered back as he pointed a finger at the house. "What's happened?"

"Can't discuss the case, sir." As the officer's words sounded, they carried a sealed black body bag from the house and Ethan fell back into a hedge. "You need to sleep it off. Where do you live?"

Ethan knew from his youth that failing to reveal his address would land him with a caution and time in a cell to get sober. "I'm just there." He pointed towards Ashleigh's bedsit and dug the key out of his pocket.

"Ease off on the booze next time."

He strolled away without causing further attention. When he glanced around, the officer was still watching him. He raised his hand and continued towards the bedsit. Ethan stepped through the bashed in door and saw Ashleigh's pink PJs folded neatly on the bed. He fell onto the bed and curled up in a ball, clutching the PJs to his face to take in her soft floral scent one last time.

Ashleigh had protected him and brought her own demise. He had to make them pay. A prison sentence wouldn't do it.

Chapter 22

Ethan's adrenaline filled hour left him trembling. He wasn't ready to say goodbye to Ashleigh, but it wouldn't be long before the police would call to check her bedsit. Wiping his eyes, he held her PJs to the side of his face for a moment longer before shoving them into a shopping bag with his stuff. He'd enough cash for a train ticket but little else, and he was starving. He checked her bedside cupboard and slipped some notes into his pocket. "Thanks Ashleigh." It felt like theft, but she'd have wanted to help him.

He needed to go, but he grabbed the frame of the door and turned back to see the bedsit. He saw the impression in the sofa from the time they'd spent together. The toaster she hadn't used since he'd fixed it. The bed they'd shared. Consumed with lament for the girl who'd given him hope, he held his head in his hands. He wanted someone's hand on his shoulder to comfort him. It didn't come.

* * *

Jennifer joined Jake at the station. She paced impatiently around the ticketing area.

"He's not coming, is he?" Jake said as Jennifer came close.

"Surely, he can't have gone back to that dingy little bedsit," Jennifer said.

"He'd already be here if he was actually coming." Jake smirked. "Did that old man send you off the trail?"

Jennifer's face boiled. "He better not have." Jennifer stormed back to the car with Jake following tight lipped.

The car pulled up outside the old man's house. "See if you can get in around the back if he gives me any trouble," Jennifer said to Jake as she opened the car. Her calm exterior from the last time she spoke to him was long gone when she knocked on the door. She looked through the window again and gave three knuckle splintering taps on the window.

The frail man stepped back into the house through the patio door and held his chest when he saw her angry face in the window. He froze with fear. Jake bursting through his garden gate broke his frightened stare as he turned and slid the glass pane across to close it. His hand turned the lock as Jake's huge hand slapped against the window. The man stumbled backwards and fell to the floor.

Jake tried the lock, then the back door, before returning to slap his hand on the patio door.

The old man was still on the floor, but had a phone in his hand.

Jake's phone rang. "Go to the bedsit through the wood. I'll drive round."

* * *

Ethan dragged himself out of the bedsit and hid from view

behind the skip. The ambulance had gone and the police officer who'd come to his aid was the last at the scene. He was contemplating whether to tell the police everything as he peered out from behind the stinking waste skip. He needed help to get justice for Ashleigh but covered in her blood and holding her clothes would land him in a prison cell.

Ethan heard a soft whispering voice which sounded like Ashleigh's, "run. run to the station." Ethan glanced around the skip but saw no-one.

To step onto the pavement would pique the interest of the officer. He needed to wait for a distraction. The distraction came as a bounding Jake burst through a bush at the side of the apartments.

"Slow down!" the officer called to him, "hey Big fella!" Jake ignored the call and crossed the road to bound up the stairs to Ashleigh's bedsit. "Assistance required," the officer hollered as she strode up the stairs.

"Run now!" the impatient whisper called. Ethan rose to his feet and took flight.

* * *

Jake turned over the sofa in annoyance, letting out a frustrated groan.

"Sir, in the house across the road, someone has committed a serious offence. I need you to calm down and answer some questions." The officer asked with her hand out, hoping to calm the beast.

"Don't think so." Jake stepped forward and before the officer could reach her taser. He picked her up and slam-dunked her over the balcony. Her game ended when her head collided with the skip. Jake descended the stairs as Jennifer arrived. He opened the car door. "We're going home. Now!"

"Not till we find Ethan." Jennifer said, following Jake's eyes to the skip.

"Collateral damage. The fuzz are going to be here any minute." Jake's stony-faced expression for once silenced Jennifer.

Three police cars entered the estate as they left it. "Forget Ethan. Get us home."

* * *

Ethan heard the sirens, but the alley had kept him out of view. Seeing Jake again had spiked his adrenaline and after sprinting clear of immediate danger, he slowed to a walk, but with his entire body shaking, he stumbled along like a drunk. Four youths saw him approaching and taunted him. "Had a few too many, mate?"

"What's in your little bag? A couple more beers," they taunted.

"No," he said, and he clenched the bag close. It held the scent of Ashleigh.

"Let's have a look then." One kid pulled at the bag and ripped it.

"What's that? A pink top." He pushed Ethan as he tried to hold the bag together.

"Got a wig in there?" Another taunted and pushed him the opposite way.

"I need your help!" Ethan said, as he stared at the leader of the taunts.

"Nearest shop is down there. Special brew's on offer." One lad said. He pushed the arm of the leader and laughed, but Ethan had maintained his desperate look.

The lead guy held his hands out and turned to his buddies. "Let the man speak." He turned back to Ethan. "Hope you've got a good story, or we'll kick the fuck out of you." The laughter erupted.

The lead held his hand up to halt the evil laughter. "Speak!"

"You couldn't take me lower if you killed me." Ethan gave them a potted version of the last day and they stopped him as he was about to mention the ditch.

"Sounds bollocks."

"The pink PJs are the only thing with her scent." Ethan sensed boots were about to fly.

With both hands and a strength, he thought had long gone, Ethan grabbed the guy's top and pulled him aggressively close. Spitting out his words, he screamed, "she's fucking dead, you prick!"

"He probably killed her after fucking her," the smallest guy said.

Ethan's faced flushed as the evil eyes returned to him. He bowed his head. "Couldn't have, even if I wanted to." Ethan pulled up his trouser leg to show the bag on his ankle.

"What the fuck is that?"

Ethan held their attention as he explained the second part of his story.

"Bullshit!"

Ethan opened his trousers to show the lead guy. He retched and turned to his buddies. "Don't look."

Ignoring the warning, they did and were also dry heaving.

"The crazy bitch that did this killed Ashleigh. I didn't go to the cops. I want to sort this myself, for Ashleigh."

"Can we help?"

"She's got a boyfriend that looks like the incredible hulk."

"Green?" the small guy asked.

"No, you idiot. He's about six foot eight and built like a tank." Ethan's retort had the guys slapping the small guy's stupid comment.

"I just need to get to the station and get back to Birmingham."

They agreed to walk with him to the station in case the hulk character was hanging around. Ethan hoped after Jake's altercation with the officer, he would be behind bars, but despite the entourage of protection, Ethan edged nervously into the ticket office. A chilly wind blew straight through his jangling bones and his twitching head checked every corner.

All was clear.

The guys who'd assaulted him stood like old friends, watching him as the train pulled away. As Ethan settled into the journey, he rested his cheek against Ashleigh's pinks and took the time to rest. With his memory now fully restored, he remembered where he lived, and he longed for the comfort of his own place. Thankfully, Jennifer didn't know where he lived, but Rachel did. Had Rachel had any part in his demise? Would he be safe to return home?

Chapter 23

Ethan changed at Birmingham New Street, and when the train pulled into his local station, the memories of his youth flooded back. He strode confidently down the high street like a returning hero, but there were no cheers to welcome him back.

His darkest memory returned as he stopped and stared from across the road at the window above the barber's. It was the flat where Jennifer had dismembered him. Tod's the barber stood innocently beneath with a young lad leant against the frame of the door waiting for an available seat.

The door leading up to Jennifer's place of hell was closed. Ethan crossed the road to get a better look at a sticker on the door. "Room to let. Ask in the barbers for information."

Ethan popped his head into Tod's. "When did the girl from upstairs move out?"

"Couple of days ago. She was two months ahead on her rent, so it must have been something unexpected. Cheeky bitch wanted a refund. I told her to piss off."

"Did she leave a forwarding address?"

"She'd not been living up there, she'd just..." he glanced at his customer in the mirror, "... been taking clients there."

The guy in the chair shook his head and gave Ethan a disapproving look through the mirror as if Ethan had been part of her antics. Ethan wanted to share the reality, but to explain exactly what she'd been doing with the 'clients,' as he'd put it, would also have highlighted he was a victim. He didn't want to be a victim anymore.

Alone with his thoughts, Ethan nearly jumped out of his skin when a tap came on his shoulder. He turned around to see a girl with flowing locks and a full smile of pearly whites. "Bit jumpy, aren't you? Ethan? The cricketer."

Despite the fright. He tried to make light of his nervousness. He stroked his chin and tilted his head. "Ruth? From the Groove?"

"Nice you remembered." Ruth smiled and ran her hand through her wavy hair and gave him a warm smile.

"Psycho girl must have got her claws into you; she didn't let you play cricket."

Ethan's eyes nearly popped out of his head. "You knew she was a psycho. Why didn't you warn me?"

She scrunched her face and shrugged. "What d'ya mean? I was just pissed you went with her."

Ethan chuckled to himself, shaking his head. "You have no idea how bad I am at choosing a girlfriend." Ethan ran both his hands through his hair and sighed. "It wasn't the click I was hoping for." It wasn't the time to reveal the extent of his tortured few weeks. He added, "she certainly changed my life."

"That's her place, isn't it?" she said, pointing to the door aside the barbers. "Are you stalking her now?"

"She's moved." Ethan gave a defensive sneer.

"To get away from you?" Ruth teased.

Ethan slowly shook his head. "Fancy a coffee."

"No can do. I'm off to work." She leant forward and gave his shoulders a warming squeeze as she planted a warming kiss on his cheek. "Hope I see you in the groove on Friday," she said as she went on her way.

Ethan watched her go, reflecting on the poor choice he'd made on that night. Ruth seemed keen, but revealing his secret would likely dampen her enthusiasm and a return to the groove was not high on his agenda.

Ethan tapped firmly on his mother's front door.

"Ethan's here," she shouted to his dad, before she flung her arms around him. "Where have you been? We've been worried sick. You could have been dead in a ditch for all we know."

Before Ethan had a chance to speak, his dad joined them. "You should know better son, we've been in pieces not knowing where you were. You were supposed to pick us up from the airport. Why didn't you answer your mobile?"

"I've not been chilling at home. You were spot on about a ditch," Ethan said.

Over a coffee, they sat in shock as Ethan shared how his world had turned upside down and how he'd joined James Walker in a ditch, but he'd been the lucky one.

His Mom had heard enough. "Are you going to the police? Or are you going to hide from them forever?"

"Going to the cops won't deliver revenge. If I ever find them, I'd like sweeter revenge than getting them locked up." Ethan clenched his fist and rested his chin on it.

"Ethan!" his dad snapped. "You should go to the police. It's over then."

"Over! Are you kidding?" Ethan flung his hands out wide. "I'd have a media circus asking me about my life without a dick and the entire world would know. It would never be over."

"How about if she does it again?"

Ethan looked into his empty coffee cup and ran his finger

around the rim. Coming to terms with what she'd done to him would never leave him, or what she'd done to Ashleigh. Prison would be too good for her and the giant, besides his only route to finding her had closed.

If he ever saw her again, he'd make sure she'd suffer like he had.

* * *

The following morning, Ethan stepped back into Bailey's Electrics. His boss, Jeff, greeted him like a long-lost son. Ethan gave him a watered-down version of his traumatic episode, telling him he'd been drugged and dropped into a ditch. Thankfully, Jeff didn't press for more detail, and Ethan was soon sitting at his bench with a faulty robot vacuum.

He welcomed the return to the mundane world of electrical repairs, but whenever the door dinged for a new customer, he twitched to alert, much to the delight of the other engineers who started calling him 'Billy Spark' as if he'd shocked himself. Ethan couldn't stop the panic which came with every bell, or the fear of seeing Jennifer's bruiser every time the door to their workshop opened.

A week later, and the jitters were no better. Ethan couldn't relax and was hardly sleeping. The Billy Spark jibes finally ceased after Jeff gave out warnings. His fellow engineers grew concerned for him. "Ethan, you really should go to the doctors and get some meds. You're not getting any better."

Ethan raised his eyes to take in their genuine concern. "I'll be fine, just no more Sparky jokes, okay." The ridicule had stopped, and they were right, meds may help, but the moment a doctor knew what had happened to him, the media circus would be in town.

"Do you want to tell us what happened to you?" one of the female engineers asked. "It may help to share."

The conversation ended as Jeff opened the door, and they hastily returned to their duties. "It's not a problem. Come on through. Ethan's in here."

Ethan grabbed a screwdriver and dashed through the fire exit. Ethan was hundred yards away when Jeff yelled, "It's Finlay from Robolicious!"

Ethan stopped and turned to see his boss and Finlay perplexed as they stood outside the fire exit. He tried to laugh it off as he trundled back with sweat dripping down his face, but their faces of concern were unmoved.

Once Finlay had left, he got called into Jeff's office and expecting repercussions for his erratic actions; he took a seat.

Jeff put a friendly arm of comfort around Ethan's nervous shoulders. "It's okay. I'm here to help." Jeff took a seat behind his desk as he continued, "I understand you've gone through something traumatic which you don't want to share, but I'm worried about you. I've called a counsellor who'll help you work through your issues."

Ethan shook his head. "I don't need a counsellor. I'll be fine."

"Ethan, you're a million miles from fine. I can't send you to New York in your current state."

Ethan snatched his desperate eyes to Jeff. "Don't cancel my trip to America."

Jeff waved his arms in the air. "I can't send you like this."

"The trip to America is the only thing keeping me sane," Ethan said, putting his hands together, pleading with his boss.

Jeff reached across the desk and placed his hand on Ethan's, and slowly shook his head.

"Someone's after me. New York is my escape," Ethan said, his eyes filling.

"What have you done?" Jeff asked. "Confession's good for the soul."

"I didn't die. That's my only sin, and some huge guy is trying to correct that. New York will give me focus and I'll come back ready to face the world again." Ethan smiled with a contrasting tear rolling down his cheek.

Jeff sat back and crossed his arms. Ethan held his stare. Jeff stroked his chin, and Ethan pulled a hopeful smile to his lips.

"Go home, take a couple of weeks off, and call me when you get to New York."

Ethan jumped to his feet, darted around the desk, and flung his arms around Jeff. "Thanks Boss."

"Get your hands off me," he said, brushing away Ethan's appreciative arms.

* * *

With some time off, Ethan reflected on how he hadn't come to the same fate as James Walker and had a second chance to do things right. Ethan headed into town to apologise to Finlay at Robolicious and collect one of the free meals he'd promised him.

"Ethan, great to see you. Come have a seat in our new premium dining area."

"Sorry about my freak out."

"It's all forgotten. Sit and relax. It's my turn to look after you."

Finlay continued to treat him like a superstar and pandered to his every need. Whether it was for the work, he'd done or because he was aware of Ethan's nervous state, Ethan didn't care. The T-Bone steak was delicious.

Nearing the bottom of a bottle of Shiraz, Ethan got to thinking about Rachel and what could have been between them. Surely, she'd calmed down and would be ready to forgive him and start over. His rose-tinted thoughts clouded over as he imagined Rachel laughing as Jennifer held up the plaque holding Ethan's severed manhood. Ethan shook his head, trying to rid the thoughts which would crush him. Jennifer didn't know where he lived, but Rachel did. If Rachel had any part in his demise, Jennifer would have been to his flat.

Finishing the wine, Ethan wondered if he was seeing things as Rachel strolled into Robolicious looking as stunning as ever in her power suit. She was no doubt celebrating another sale. He stood and waved before stepping down to greet her.

Rachel didn't smile when she spotted him, but she didn't frown, either. Perhaps she'd found out he'd done nothing wrong, and she was ready to welcome him back. Ethan held his arms out wide to welcome an embrace.

Rachel stepped closer and held his chin. "Sober up, loser." A swift knee in his balls followed. "Stay the fuck away from me."

Bent double on the floor, clenching his balls, Finlay's was the next voice he heard as he crouched beside him. "I think you need to re-think your chat up lines. What the hell did you say to her?"

* * *

Safely back in his flat, Ethan called his old buddy Mirek. Mirek had been a great friend to him during the four years they spent at Manchester University. They'd shared digs and, thanks to Mirek's charm, they'd had a regular supply of girls back to their place. Ethan had been a willing wingman as Mirek rifled through an endless supply of girls. It had been a fruitful time for the otherwise awkward and more studious Ethan.

"I'll send you a picture, Goldie is a beauty. I took her on as a secretary, but she took down more than just my notes. So, I'm promoting her to the position of my wife."

"What happened to playing the field?"

"Been there, done that. Time to settle down."

Ethan opened the picture to see the curly golden-haired beauty with mesmerizing green eyes and full baby pink lips. "She looks like a gold digger."

"Don't say that."

"Am I right in saying business is good?"

"Business is excellent. Got some big clients now. We've just clinched the marketing contract for the Tushi Corporation."

Ethan's ears pricked up at the mention of Tushi. "Can you put in a word for me?"

"Its early days yet. Let me get the first year out of the way before I ask them for favours. Enough about work. You need to meet Goldie. She's a genuine treasure."

"I bet you've flowered her with treats with the money flowing in."

Mirek mumbled, "one or two."

"Let me check out her credentials and see if she's for keeps when I'm back from New York. You know I'm an excellent judge of character." Ethan smiled to himself, knowing he was no better than Mirek.

"That'll be too late. We're getting married in two weeks. We're flying out to Vegas."

"And I thought I'd be your best man." Ethan laughed. "Just kidding, have fun."

Chapter 24

After everything he'd suffered, the time in America would give Ethan a chance to be normal and not have to look over his shoulder every five minutes. The month of study at the school of Artificial Intelligence and Robotics was a fitting thanks from his boss for getting the lucrative contract with Robolicious. Ethan gladly accepted, knowing a recommendation from Professor Artemis would give him a splendid chance to work with the Tushi Corporation. It was a strange gift from his boss, but perhaps Jeff knew Ethan was destined for more and wanted to help him rather than hinder him, not that a contact inside Tushi would be a bad thing. The Tushi Corporation were at the forefront of house bot development and artificial intelligence. Ethan wanted to be a part of it.

Ethan had read about Professor Artemis who was experimenting with enhancements which would enable quantum technology to work with artificial intelligence to create a droid brain which would perform better than its human counterpart. For future work, he'd stated, one day we will also enhance the human brain by using a computational interface fitted directly onto the brain.

Arriving in New York was a new beginning for Ethan and a chance to study without the distraction of sex, which blighted his college days, but on his very first day, a young woman with blond bobbed hair drew his attention.

She introduced herself to the class. "Hi, I'm Chloe, I've recently completed my MSc in Robotics with Artificial Intelligence and I'm an apprentice engineer at the Tushi Corporation in the UK," she said with a confident English accent, without sounding brash. She looked around at the other students and gave a coy smile in Ethan's direction before she re-took her seat. Ethan tingled all over. If he'd a penis, it would have stood to attention.

"Marry me," Ethan said under his breath. She was the most beautiful woman he'd ever seen with the brains to match. Hopefully, he could get friendly with her and switch off the usual patter, which often failed. Maybe lacking his manhood may actually prevent him from talking with his dick.

On Ethan's turn, he said, "I'm Ethan, looking to develop my knowledge of robotics and help the Tushi Corporation to design the ultimate AI droid." Chloe was looking in his direction, as were the rest of the class, but he held his gaze on the Professor.

Mentioning Tushi had been the hook, which prompted the question at the end of the lecture. Ethan had been scribbling his last few notes when Chloe asked, "Do you work at Tushi? I haven't seen you there."

Ethan looked up, and his mouth was like a sandpit. She was even more perfect at close quarters. "Not yet," he mumbled, "but that's where I want to be." Ethan avoided the cheesy smile, which usually followed when he spoke with an attractive woman. After his initial mumble, he did his best to appear calm. "I bet it's an interesting place to work."

"Yep, it sure is. If someone's going to take over the world, you want to be on their side."

Ethan nodded, stuck for words.

"Fancy getting a coffee?" Chloe asked.

Ethan nearly fainted. Gorgeous girls didn't ask him for coffee. They may ask him to get one for them. He nearly responded as if she had, but he grabbed his study notes. "My shout."

Despite working for Tushi, Chloe had very little hands-on experience. Ethan impressed Chloe when he told her about fixing the droids in the Robo-restaurant. "Sounds like you're more than ready for Tushi. Shall I put a word in for you? Okzu wants me to work on the development team for the next level droids."

"You've spoken to Okzu Tushi." Ethan couldn't contain his excitement.

Chloe shrugged like it was no big deal. "Okzu's spoken to me loads of times. I could mention you when I get back. With your experience, you'd be a great addition to the team." She smiled. "You could help me."

"Sounds like a splendid plan." Ethan smiled, holding back from the full-on hug and kiss he wanted to give her.

* * *

Over the four weeks, Ethan and Chloe became best buddies.

"I wasn't sure about you to begin with. I thought you'd try to hit on me, but after a month you haven't tried it on at all. Now, I'm kinda disappointed. Do you have a girlfriend or boyfriend back home?"

Having spent the month getting to know her, it came out of the blue. Ethan gave her a sideward glance.

"I knew it. You're gay, aren't you? My mates said you would

be."

"Did you assume if I was straight, I wouldn't have been able to resist you?" Ethan said, his tongue firmly in his cheek.

Chloe's cheeks burned bright. "I'm sorry. You must think I'm terrible, a right pretentious prom-queen, but I've been flirting with you for the entire month. I was sure you were gay."

Ethan couldn't tease her anymore. He put his hand on her shoulder. "Sorry to disappoint you and your buddies. I'm straight."

"So, you don't fancy me then." She pursed her bottom lip and looked so cute he wanted to tear off her clothes right there in the café.

"You're okay I guess." If he'd been Pinocchio, he'd have used his nose for pole-vaulting.

"You've got to like me more than that," she said, giving him her cutest smile as she made a circle with her index finger on his knee

Ethan somehow kept his nonchalant pretence and held out his open hand, gesturing it was an even chance, to which Chloe jabbed a tickling finger into his ribs. Ethan laughed and returned the favour. In the resulting melee, Chloe's half-finished coffee smashed on the floor, much to the displeasure of the middle-aged barista, who shouted them out of sight. Still giggling, they arrived at their hotel. "You wanna come to my room?" Chloe asked.

Ethan couldn't turn down the offer, but made light of her request. "I hope you're not just after me for my body."

Chloe glanced at his groin. "It's okay. I noticed the catheter bag."

Ethan took the casual comment like it was a heavyweight

boxer's haymaker. A gentle draft would have sent him crashing to the canvas.

"I like you. I'm not just after your dick."

Ethan recovered from his mental stumble. "Glad to hear it." He was indeed overwhelmingly pumped to hear it.

"I'd settle for a bedtime kiss."

Ethan walked her to her room, and they ordered a bottle of wine and chatted till the early hours about how Ethan had lost his "little soldier" as Chloe put it.

For the first time, Ethan was almost glad he didn't have a penis. There's no way he would have courted Chloe properly, with a raging appendage wanting attention. Having played it cool for an entire month, he was into the platonic routine, as James would have put it. When Chloe let out a subtle yawn, Ethan got up from the bed they'd been chatting on. "Guess I'd better let you get some sleep. Early flight tomorrow."

"I thought you'd promised me a goodnight kiss," Chloe said, puckering up for him.

To have such a beauty laying on her hotel bed, enticing him to kiss her, would have been a dream come true for virtually any bloke, but having formed a great connection with her, he was nervous to spoil it. Especially as she'd promised to put in a word for him with Okzu Tushi.

The thought of James Walker shaking his head came to mind, and Ethan swore he could feel James push him back towards the bed.

"It's fine, if you're gay." She said before turning away and sitting on the edge of the bed.

Ethan was eager to assure her he was straight, but when she pulled her top off, words would not appear. She slipped her bra off, undid her belt, and bent away from him for erotic effect as she slid her jeans over her cute rear. She glanced around to catch his mouth wide open and his eyes fixed on her ass. "I guess you're straight then."

"Yes, I'm straight," he said, lost in his admiration of her rear.

She grabbed her cotton nightdress and slipped it over her head, giving him a deliberate glimpse of her breasts as she turned back around to face him. "Just shy then, after losing your little soldier?" she asked with a teasing smile.

"I guess," he mumbled.

With a confident strut, she made her way around the bed to him and pointed her finger teasingly at him. "You've missed the opportunity to kiss me goodnight, but you've seen me naked now." She tapped his nose with her finger.

He froze on the spot as she undid the top button of his shirt and the next. She leant in close and gave him a kiss on his cheek. He turned his head to kiss her, but she put a single finger to his lips. She undid another button and kissed his neck. Another button popped open, and she kissed the top of his chest. Opening the remaining buttons, she nibbled his single nipple and looked up for his reaction.

Ethan was tingling all over, including his balls, which had awoken from their retired state. With his arms at his side unable to respond, she slipped his open shirt off his shoulders to the floor. His hands stopped her when she slipped the belt out of its buckle.

"It's too late for you to go back to your room," she said with her hand on his belt.

He wanted to answer that he was only six doors down the corridor.

"Will you lie down with me?" she asked as she dipped her

head down and looked up at him.

He'd been coy about getting into bed with Ashleigh after concealing his catheter, but Chloe already knew about everything. "Do you just want to see?"

She stepped back and pulled back the duvet. "I can't say I'm not intrigued, but I just wanted you to join me in bed. I'm obviously not after intercourse." She rolled her eyes and shook her head.

Ethan heard the voice of James Walker in his head saying, get in there, you idiot. Ethan smiled to himself. Chloe had a fantastic mind and the body to match. He stepped up to Chloe and took her in his arms, as they shared the most magical of kisses, before he took his own trousers off to join her beneath the covers.

Chapter 25

Chloe awoke first and snuggled closer to Ethan, resting her head on his chest. She loved to hear the beating of his heart as his chest rose and fell. Ethan was a step above the usual jerks Chloe had been with. Most guys ignored the fact she had a brain. They tried to impress her with their muscles and a jackhammer action in bed.

Sure, sex with them had been good, but she strived for a deeper connection. Although Ethan was definitely in beta male territory, she loved his caring and composed manner. He opened doors for her and pulled her chair out. Several blokes had done that for a week to impress her, only to turn into a regular jerk off after bedding her. Ethan clearly hadn't done it to get her into bed.

As she'd got to know him, she realized it was his way; he was courteous to everyone, but what inspired her most of all was the way his mind worked and the ideas he had for Tushi.

She considered if he was only being nice to her to get a job at Tushi, but the way he'd excelled in their classes, Professor Artemis would call Okzu, anyway. He'd also be a great perk in her struggle to add physical application to her knowledge. Cameron was Chloe's supervisor. She'd put up with his leering, so long as he didn't touch her, because after failing every practical test, without Cameron's support, they'd have kicked her off the programme.

When she'd got called into Cameron's office, she assumed it was to let her go, but the course in NYC with Professor Artemis seemed to be her last chance to get herself in gear. The admiring glance from Ethan gave her the opportunity to get help to pass the course. When she spotted the catheter bag protruding from his trouser leg, it held the excuse to avoid intimacy and focus on her studies, but when she found out what a great guy he was, her heart went out to him.

Chloe gently woke Ethan by tickling his nipple with her tongue and stroking her hand over his chest before she gave him a warm kiss. "Morning."

"Morning, beautiful," Ethan replied, his hand pulling her close again to take in her natural scent.

Chloe rested her head back on his chest and put her arm over his chest to cuddle him. She reflected on the previous night and how they'd cuddled and kissed. She'd felt his firm yet tender touch over her body, but much to her disappointment, he'd not put his hand between her legs. He'd been a perfect gentleman, content to hold her in his embrace, apart from a brief squeeze of her bum.

After being horny the previous night and not getting a release, she awoke with the same feeling. She could have sorted herself out, but she wanted Ethan to play his part, despite not having all the equipment. She was also keen to get a look at his groin.

She asked rather sheepishly as she gave his nipple a gentle squeeze. "Can I look at your groin?"

Ethan rolled his eyes. "I feel like a circus attraction."

She sat up like a shot, giving him a beaming smile as she clapped her hands together.

"There's not much to see," Ethan said.

Ethan pulled his boxers down a little, but Chloe pulled the duvet off his legs and pulled his boxers all the way off.

Chloe responded to his reddening cheeks. "It's okay. I'll be gentle." She rested her hands on his knees and gave him a caring smile. "Close your eyes," she said with authority.

Ethan put his hands behind his head and did as she instructed.

Chloe wanted to comment on the horror he'd experienced, but didn't mention it, not wanting to draw an early conclusion to her investigation. She lifted his knees up and asked him to open his legs.

"Tell me what you can feel," she asked.

"My legs are cool, but my face is burning."

"Relax," her delicate voice whispered. "Can you feel my hands?"

"You've got them on my knees. I'm not paralysed," Ethan said sarcastically.

"Good boy." She kissed the inside of each knee and knelt down between his legs to look closely at the stitching.

She stroked the back of her index finger slowly up the side of his scrotum, and Ethan let out a long sigh of pleasure. "That's a nice tickle."

A gentle flick of the catheter tube made him flinch.

"You felt that then," she said. "How about this?"

Her warm breath near the base of the protruding tube got another reaction. "I got to feel that."

Chloe got closer still and tickled her tongue around the side of the tube. Ethan's breath hitched. "Is that good?" Chloe asked, knowing the answer.

"Not sure. Do it again," Ethan said with a smile on his face.

173

Chloe grinned at Ethan's expression before returning with a kiss and a suck to the flesh around the tube.

"That's fantastic." Ethan ran his fingers through her hair.

"Don't freak out," Chloe said as she teased a finger around and into his behind.

* * *

Ethan hadn't favoured the method, but the orgasm felt mighty good.

"Good boy. My tests are complete." Chloe said.

Ethan's brow creased. "I thought you were pleasuring me."

"I was. You liked it, didn't you?" Chloe said, pointing an accusatory finger.

"Of course, I did, just didn't think it would feel so good."

"For a smart guy, you have some gaps in your sexual knowledge. I guess you haven't had a long-term partner to experiment with."

"Not really, no." Ethan screwed his face up.

Chloe shook her head. "Ethan, keep up. You can ejaculate, which means if we can get you a new penis, you're back in business."

Ethan rolled his eyes. "Shall we pop to the supermarket before we go to the airport?"

"Or create one at Tushi." Chloe's big blue eyes sparkled with excitement.

Ethan put his hands on her shoulders, his face serious. "Do you think that's possible?"

"Anything's possible at Tushi."

Ethan pulled Chloe in close. "You are a smart cookie." Ethan

174

then delivered some tickles to her waist. Chloe screamed enough to wake the whole of the hotel, but neither of them cared.

Chloe wriggled free and off the bed before returning to sit astride Ethan and with her lips full of passion, she kissed Ethan and they cuddled in loving bliss.

"I wish I could give you more," Ethan said.

"You've got a mouth and fingers. How about returning the favour?" Chloe asked with an expectant glare before pointing both hands at her peach panties.

"I can have a go. Not very experienced, though."

"Don't worry, I'll tell you if you're not doing it right."

Ethan rolled Chloe over onto her back and with Chloe as his guide, he fully returned the favour Chloe wanted.

After showering together and enjoying each soapy touch of Chloe's body, Ethan collected his things from his room and hand in hand, they took the lift and stepped into a transport pod to take them to the airport.

Chapter 26

Chloe did as she promised and arranged for Ethan to have an informal meeting with her supervisor, Cameron.

Ethan knew it didn't guarantee him a job, but getting on with Cameron would be a step in the right direction. He put aside the annoyance built from what Chloe had said about his questionable behaviour.

"Ethan, thanks for coming in." Cameron's firm handshake and square jaw confirmed he was an alpha male type who usually got everything he wanted from women, or anyone else. He was a tall, blond-haired guy who was no stranger to the gym. He led Ethan through to the canteen area and without asking if Ethan drank coffee, pressed the machine for a couple of coffees.

Cameron passed a coffee to Ethan. "Is coffee okay?" Ethan thanked him with a polite nod, before Cameron continued, "you'll need lots of coffee working here, especially if you're working with Chloe."

Ethan gave another polite nod. His newfound love of Chloe called for a rebuke, but it wasn't the time for grand gestures. Cameron was talking as if Ethan joining the team had already received approval.

"Professor Artemis spoke well of you, and it seems Chloe is also keen to work with you. I just need to see if I can get it bought off by Okzu Tushi."

The anticipation of an offer had filled Ethan's chest with hope, but hearing Cameron hadn't spoken with Okzu Tushi let all his optimism leave him with a long sigh he couldn't disguise.

"I hope Chloe didn't say it was a done deal."

"It's an informal chat, that's all," Ethan replied. He could hardly tell him that Chloe had said the position was all but his.

"I hope it's more than that. We are in the early stages of a project which has the potential to change the world. We need smart guys like you."

Ethan sipped his coffee, trying to appear cool, taking in such a statement. "Sounds like something I'd like to be involved with." Ethan put his coffee down and straightened in his seat, holding his head up with pride as an optimistic air filled his lungs. Cameron smirked and relaxed into his seat, and took another sip of his coffee.

Like the police had burst into a squat, Cameron sat bolt upright and returned his coffee to the table like it was an illegal substance. He quickly stood to attention, and Ethan turned to see what had caused such a reaction.

"Cameron! Slacking again!" snapped the genius, Okzu Tushi with two eight feet tall guardian bots aside him.

"Not at all, Mr Tushi. I have a candidate for the new programme." Cameron's words sped out like he'd get shot if he dared to dawdle.

Ethan followed suit and stood straight with his chest puffed out.

"Speak!" Okzu Tushi boomed at Cameron.

"This is Ethan, he comes recommended by Professor Artemis," Cameron answered like a scolded child apologising for lateness.

"Artemis!"

"Yes, Mr Tushi. He could help Chloe." Cameron's voice slowed to a more relaxed speed.

"Application Ethan! Do you have any experience?"

Despite his heart beating out of his chest, Ethan spoke with a calmness Cameron would never have, replying like a grand master. "I've spent three years repairing Robot Vacuums." The nostrils of Mr Tushi took in air, ready to deliver judgement, but Ethan calmly continued, "I recently fixed the service robots at the Robo-restaurant, Robolicious."

Ethan froze as Mr Tushi stepped closer to Ethan and put his index finger under Ethan's chin as he looked deep into his eyes. "You have a kind soul." Mr Tushi stepped back but kept his eye on Ethan. "Cameron, introduce him to the team."

"Yes, Mr Tushi," Cameron said, bowing his head and stepping back.

Okzu Tushi went on his way, with his protection bots following close behind.

Cameron patted Ethan on the shoulder. "Great interview."

Ethan snapped his head back to Cameron and raised his hands aloft. "Was that it?"

"Yep. Okzu is very much about sensing the soul of people. He must like you, he sent away the last three Artemis recommended. Welcome on board."

* * *

Ethan had seen the clunky house bots on TV ads and had completed simple fixes to the shiny bots at Robolicious, but to be working on them for real gave new meaning to his life, and he loved the prospect of developing them further.

Cameron walked Ethan around the facility. Ethan asked questions at every turn, impressed by the plans the company had and the size of the planned operation. The Tushi corporation was only a medium-sized company, but with the plans for exponential growth and the advancements they were developing, the Tushi bots would be more advanced than anything else on the market. It was the perfect time to join the company.

Assigned to support Chloe with designing the coverall skin for the next update, Ethan was directly into the action and the problem solving he enjoyed. The pliability of the skin struggled around the main joints, but combining an elastic membrane inside the joint enabled them to pull back into position to maintain the realism of the movements. It was a significant upgrade, replacing the latex pads and shiny joints.

After several months of overcoming endless issues, they finally cracked it and received approval from quality control. They achieved sign off in time for the quarterly briefing. Chloe commented they may get a mention, but when Okzu wasn't there, the praise fell flat.

Ethan wanted to get more involved in the mechanical and software side of things. He befriended a programmer and with their help snuck in to observe a test run of the early stage artificial intelligence, which would enable the bots to learn quicker and become more useful in the home.

The lead demonstrator explained, "the crucial element is how to control learning ability. Unrestricted deep learning would be a concern. The program limits their learning to improving home life interactions and provides the best support for their families, without getting ideas above their station."

Ethan raised his hand for a question and promptly received a dig in the ribs. The guy who'd let him in discreetly pulled him to the back of the room. The meeting had engrossed Ethan, but the maddened face of the guy reminded him he hadn't received an invite and shouldn't have been there.

"Do you want us both thrown out the window?" he said through gritted teeth. "Hope Okzu didn't spot you," he said, shaking his head and directing Ethan out of the access door.

* * *

Enjoying his time with both Chloe and Tushi, Ethan was on cloud nine as the day he'd most looked forward to finally arrived. The annual message from Okzu Tushi.

"Come on! We want a good spot for the presentation," Ethan said as he pulled Chloe by the hand.

"It's just a business update," Chloe said, trying to pull Ethan back to a regular pace.

"We'll get a big announcement. I'm sure of it." Ethan said. "I'll ask him about the deep learning, if he doesn't mention it."

Chloe gave Ethan a firm tug. "Don't ask questions," she said through gritted teeth, before they stepped through the frosted glass door into the conference room.

Ethan pulled her in closer. "Why? I'm buzzing with questions already." Ethan had been like a kid in a toy shop for three months. Every new discovery had him gaping with amazement.

"Ethan!" she whispered. "The last guy that asked a question

got thrown out of a window." Chloe's blank expression told him she wasn't joking.

Ethan put his hand over his mouth before sliding it down to his chin to reveal a cheesy grin.

"Fine. If that's how you want to end it," Chloe said, shaking her head at Ethan's boundless enthusiasm before her lips curled into a smile.

The room filled with Engineers and had an excitable buzz until the first protection droid ducked its head and entered the room. When Okzu Tushi strolled in, a polite ripple of applause broke out. The second protection bot followed him into the room. Okzu raised his hand, and the applause stopped with the efficiency of an orchestral pause, but with one exception, Cameron had taken his eyes off Okzu and added a final solitary clap.

Stern-faced Okzu fixed a stare on him for a few seconds before a smile returned. He surveyed the room like he was glancing into the soul of every attendee. He nodded to his assistant and said, "begin," as he calmly stepped to the side of the screen which filled half the wall.

The presentation showed the financials, before Okzu detailed the plans for the next few years. Ethan and Chloe's work got a mention, and a polite ripple of appreciation followed.

Okzu raised his hand to halt the applause. It duly stopped dead with Cameron holding Okzu's stare. Okzu delivered the next part of the brief.

"Ethan and Chloe's work was the beginning. The next stage is human looking imitation skin, but we are not stopping there.

"Trials in the lab have confirmed we can now grow human skin without a host and will soon grow it on the house bot endoskeleton. Future house bots will look like humans.

"The silicon skin is limited and prevents a full range of expressions on our droids. During stage two, we will switch out the artificial skin on the heads for living tissue to enable the house bots to better assimilate with their human counterparts."

There was a murmur in the group.

"Silence!" Okzu shouted and the protection droids walked amongst those who'd dared to distract themselves from the message.

"Anyone not happy with the direction of the business. We have an opening," he paused for effect, "window."

"I think it's awesome." Ethan's faced beamed with his chest out, whilst Chloe held her forehead, expecting the worst, but Okzu ignored Ethan's comment and continued with the presentation.

"Great work on the skin, Ethan," an engineer said as they filed out.

"I helped too," Chloe snapped, with a stare in their direction.

"Yep, it was a team effort." Ethan took Chloe's hand and filed off towards the skin modelling office.

"Looks like you got away with your little stunt in the AI programming lab," Chloe said, giving Ethan a sideward glance.

"How did you know about that?" Ethan frowned.

"Heard about it from a couple of guys. You were lucky Okzu didn't see you." Chloe gestured with her finger slashing across her throat.

* * *

A year later and Ethan's work had gained company-wide appreciation. Dave Winston, the design & engineering manager, who had been with Okzu from the start of the UK operation, took Ethan under his wing. Ethan had taken on more responsibility and spent less time with Chloe in the skin lab, focusing more on the AI programming lab. Chloe didn't seem to mind and had become more confident in her role, thanks to Ethan. She'd also moved in with Ethan and they had a great relationship, despite Ethan's missing appendage.

Ethan had been on cloud nine, but rumours of a big announcement had caused tension with him and Dave Winston. "I don't know what you're worried about. Okzu has steered the company amazingly well. Trust him!"

"You're under his bloody spell, like everyone else. He thinks he can control everything. The bots help people not replace them."

Dave's outburst surprised Ethan. He'd always been behind everything Okzu had done. Ethan probed for more information, but Dave remained tight-lipped on the detail.

The next company message from Okzu Tushi arrived and with rumours rife, there was a buzz of anticipation.

After the usual turnover and profit reporting had shown the continued growth of the company, the screen displayed, "and now for the big news."

Okzu stepped in front of the screen. He raised his hand to stop the excited murmurings and silence immediately fell. "I have some splendid news. My long-term plans for the Tushi Corporation are now taking shape. I'm in final stage talks for the acquisition of the Japanese sex bot company, Joi." Okzu nodded his head towards Dave Winston.

Dave stepped towards the screen as it showed a presentation of the Joi business. "As you can see, Company Joi has been remarkably successful, building and selling realistic sex dolls. Joi has a lot of intellectual property for the sex organs which we could use, hence the acquisition." Dave gave a slight shrug, bringing a frown from Okzu.

Dave rolled his eyes, and Okzu's face boiled. "Enough! That! Will be all," Okzu enunciated every word with a sinister prominence which put the room on edge.

Dave's eyes shifted uneasily as a protection bot gestured for him to leave the room.

Okzu let out a heavy, displeasing sigh. "Wait in my office," Okzu said calmly and deliberately. The room knew Dave's time was up.

Okzu paused whilst Dave left the room with his protection bot.

"When the takeover is complete. We will start work on understanding the technology and how we can incorporate it into our own machines. Joi's engineers are part of the deal and will support our learning curve until we introduce the jewel in the Tushi crown, Tushi Wives. We will combine house bot technology with the sex bots to create an artificially intelligent droid that can cook, clean, and then provide all the love and sex their owner's desire. We will of course also produce Tushi Hubbies for the single ladies, but they will be secondary as we expect less demand."

At the end of the presentation, Chloe and Ethan filed out with the rest of the engineers. "Sounds fantastic," Ethan said.

An engineer in ear shot responded, "Engineers from Joi, coming here. Looks like more of us will join Dave out the window."

"He won't throw Dave out the window," Ethan said casually.

"You reckon. I think you've still got plenty to learn about

Okzu. Here's my advice, never cross Okzu Tushi?" another engineer said.

The following day, word had got around about the demise of Dave Winston and with the engineering manager gone, rumours of a manager from Joi appearing were rife through the department.

Ethan saw the positive side of things and was looking forward to working with someone new. Chloe suggested the new guy may be able to make him a new penis as they headed home for a relaxing evening. Chloe sorted a gourmet meal which arrived by drone before a romantic movie and cuddles followed.

Chapter 27

Ethan delivered a sustained assault of tickles the following morning, which resulted in a shared shower and a late start to the day. Ethan's life was progressing well. He had the love of the sensational Chloe and the best job in the world. The chances of getting a replacement for his missing penis would receive a massive boost if the acquisition of company Joi completed, not that he'd particularly missed it with the multiple joys of the flesh he shared with Chloe.

Sneaking in nearly an hour late, Chloe was full of giggles as they tried to avoid meeting Cameron on the way to the design room.

"Made it." Chloe giggled as she shut the door behind Ethan, and they checked on the final endurance testing for the joints. The physical test had run for the equivalent of five years' movement and was now deteriorating. Three years would have sufficed, so every day was a bonus. They cut short their celebrations when a heavy knock hit the door.

After pushing open the door, the protection bot crouched its head and stepped inside. "You have a meeting with Okzu Tushi. Come this way."

"Okzu? I don't have a meeting with Okzu." Despite the progress Ethan had made, he'd never been in a meeting or even spoken with him.

"He doesn't book meetings with his employees. If he wants you, you go immediately," Chloe said. The colour on her face from their fun-filled morning faded to grey.

"You have a meeting with Okzu Tushi. Come this way." The bot repeated politely as it held the door open.

"See you later," Ethan said with a nervous smile. The deathly expression on Chloe's face didn't reassure him.

The bot stopped at an unmarked door and held its metallic palm to the access pad. An electronic click followed, and the door smoothly opened to reveal a service lift. The bot stepped back and placed a guiding, yet insistent nudge into Ethan's back.

Ethan had experienced his fair share of torture and stepping into the unknown again made his pulse race. The bot followed him into the security lift, pulled the caged door down, selected the top button, and stepped back as the lift slowly ascended. The dimly lit lift made the protection bot all the more menacing, and the eerie silence from it didn't help. Ethan tried to make light of the situation. "I guess you don't get the personality upgrades."

The bot snatched its head towards Ethan, its piercing red eyes fixed on him.

"Or the humour then." Ethan asked, outwardly confident but inwardly shitting himself.

The bot's eyes remained fixed on Ethan.

Some people would judder and shake with the thought of facing the wrath of Okzu, but Ethan figured anything after the ditch was an extension to his life and he wouldn't let fear consume him. As the lift continued its rise, Ethan tested the bot further. "I like what you've done with your hair," as he pointed to the bot's shiny steel head.

The bot turned its head, looking for what Ethan had pointed out, before touching its head and slowly turning its head to re-focus on Ethan.

Ethan had run out of quips and breathed a sigh of relief when the lift came to a stop, but the bot's eyes ignored the lift and remained focused on Ethan. "You make jokes when you are nervous."

Ethan returned a grin, hoping the capability for aggression from the bot wouldn't appear.

Without a further word, the bot turned its head to the cage door, lifted it with one strong hand, before stepping out and scanning the access door.

Ethan followed the bot through into a show of opulence. Blood red carpeting, running along a well-lit corridor with gold leaf framed paintings and antique vases of obvious value. He stopped to admire a Chinese chess set (bronze and silver) in a glass case. Another shove in his back reminded him it was not a sightseeing visit.

Turning into another corridor, two more protection bots stood outside a wooden door. Ethan's guide said pointed to the door and continued on its way. Ethan looked the carved mahogany door up and down, taking in the majestic image of a Chinese dragon in a garden.

The protection bots didn't engage with Ethan standing like statues on either side of the door. Ethan was about to knock on the door, as one bot spoke. "Wait!" Ethan froze with his fist hovering a fraction away from the door.

"Enter!" the bot said as the door opened itself. Ethan stepped forward to see Okzu. He was staring at one of his two desk monitors from behind his imposing yet virtually empty desk.

Ethan glanced back as the door closed behind him.

Surely, Okzu hadn't called him to his office over his late appearance that morning. Cameron would have been more than appropriate to deliver a dressing down for poor timekeeping.

He berated himself for the poor choices he continued to make, but he couldn't resist checking out the progress of the new plasma battery production area, which Dave had kept to himself and refused to let Ethan get involved with. Surely Okzu wouldn't criticize him for his inquisitive nature. It would be ridiculous to lose his job for showing a healthy, or arguably unhealthy, interest in departments which were nothing to do with him. It was no cause for a firing, but Okzu had not yet showed any sign of compassion for his employees.

"Ethan. Take a seat." Okzu said, stepping through Ethan's tortured thoughts.

Chapter 28

Remorse is good. Maybe that'll save him. "First, I'd like to apologise-"

Okzu raised his hand and Ethan stopped mid-sentence.

"I know you were late this morning."

Ethan wanted to apologise, but didn't dare interrupt.

"I noticed you were in a relationship with Chloe, despite a missing appendage."

It stunned Ethan. How could Okzu have known? His cheeks reddened at the sensitive information being revealed.

"I also spotted you in the new production area, for which you have no access."

Okzu paused, but Ethan could not speak. No word of apology or explanation would save him. Maybe he should have stayed in the ditch. Bloody idiot. This is the best job ever, and he'd messed it up.

Were Okzu's guardians going to pull his arms and legs off before tossing him out of the window? From the mischievous smirk growing on Okzu's face, it appeared he enjoyed torturing people. Ethan shook his head at what a waste it would be if he'd come all the way from the ditch to have his life end because of an overzealous interest in his work.

Okzu grinned.

Ethan guessed the window would provide a swift end to it all. He snapped out of his malaise to plead his case. "Okzu. I love this company. I want to be involved in every single part of it."

Okzu crossed his arms, his expression blank.

"I will do anything I can to make this happen for you." Ethan meant every word.

Okzu's poker face held.

Ethan held back from a further plea and held Okzu's gaze.

Okzu strolled around his desk with his hands behind his back. He continued around the back of Ethan, who twisted his neck to keep Okzu in his sight. The menacing silence felt like a thousand blades which could shoot through him any second. Ethan spun his head back around as Okzu passed by him and returned to his desk.

Ethan wanted to plead again for a reprieve, but his throat caught his words.

"Ethan. You have a kind soul. I like you."

Ethan returned a nervous smile. If Okzu followed it with a but, he would jump out of the window himself to avoid the emotional torture of his last day being drawn out for some evil pleasure.

"Ethan, you've performed exceptionally well since you joined my company. Your current role is not enough for you, I can see that. As you may have heard, Dave Winston is no longer our Design & Engineering Manager. I'd like you to take the position."

Chills ran straight through Ethan like a winter gale. He hoped it didn't show and stood with a confidence which James Walker would have been proud of; he put his right hand forward across Okzu's desk. "It would be my pleasure."

Okzu shook his hand with a knowing grin. "You have a lot to learn, but I will guide you. We can build this company together."

Bearing in mind, Ethan thought he was about to be given a drop to his death. His face of relief beamed. He continued to shake the hand of his tormentor and mentally restored Okzu to the pedestal he'd created for him. Ethan couldn't contain his excitement at having Okzu as his mentor.

A firm vice-like grip from Okzu told Ethan to loosen, which he did. Okzu wiped the clammy feel from Ethan's hand on a napkin pulled from a drawer as he continued. "Nakamori Shinto from Joi will be here next week. He'll provide the support for you to manage the transition."

"The deal's done." Ethan's face lit up like a headlight. "Fantastic!"

"I completed the finer details yesterday," Okzu said nonchalantly, as if there had never been a doubt.

"I'm looking forward to seeing the detail on the sexual organs. I hear they are outstanding," Ethan said whilst thinking about the possibility of having a new dick fitted.

"He will also work with you to create a replacement for your missing appendage," Okzu said as if Ethan had spoken his thoughts out loud.

"How did you know about that?" Ethan answered without thinking.

Okzu stepped back wide eyed.

"I make it a priority to know everything about my employees."

It was hardly an answer to Ethan's abrupt question, but he had no intention of asking again, and Okzu was unlikely to elaborate.

* * *

Ethan burst back through the skin lab door, and Chloe snatched her head to see his cheesy grin. She jumped to her feet and dived into his arms. They held each other's embrace as the emotion of the morning slowly came out. Ethan released first at the sniffling from Chloe. Her eyes were full.

"I didn't think I'd see you again." She wiped her eyes with the back of her hand and gave an embarrassed smile.

"All is good," Ethan said. He held his hands out wide and puffed out his chest as he grinned. "I'm a survivor."

Chloe rested her forehead against his shoulder, and his arms comforted her. "I thought you were a dead man for sure." She sniffled again and wiped her nose. "How did you talk your way out of it?"

"Far from it. He knew about us, about us being late and my sneaky visit into the plasma battery area. Okzu knows everything." Ethan glanced down at his groin and returned his attention to Chloe. "Everything."

Chloe's brow creased. "So, why did he call you to his office?"

"He wants me to be the new Design & Engineering Manager. Dave Winston has gone."

Like being hit with a shock wave, Chloe jumped back ten feet and backed up till she reached the wall. Her face pale and her eyes wide open like she'd seen a ghost.

"What's the matter? It is excellent news. Okzu is going to mentor me."

"Talk about making a deal with the devil."

"He's not that bad. I'm sure he'll be fine when I get to know him better."

Chloe shook her head. "Did you forget he just had your predecessor killed for disagreeing with his intended direction of the company?"

"I agree with the direction. It'll be fine."

Ethan explained about the forthcoming arrival of Nakamori Shinto and how he'd be working with him to integrate the technical aspects from the sex bots to prepare for the launch of the Tushi wives and the Tushi hunks. It was an exciting time for the company. When Ethan shared the news Shinto would also help to develop a replacement for his penis, Chloe realised nothing could dent Ethan's enthusiasm.

"I guess it's all good news for you. Who's going to help me if you bugger off to run the entire company with Okzu?" Chloe screwed her face up in fake annoyance.

"I'm never going to be far from you. You're still my world." Ethan took Chloe's face in his hands and delivered a loving kiss to reassure her nothing would change between them.

* * *

That evening, Chloe tried to talk to Ethan. "I hope you realise there's no turning back. Okzu will expect you to do everything he wants. Dave Winston hadn't had a holiday in ten years."

"You worry too much. Once I've got a new penis, we can take a holiday and test it out."

"What makes you think I want you to test it out on me?" she teased.

"I'm not getting one for anyone else."

"Ooh! I am honoured," Chloe said, before rolling her eyes and laying her head back onto his lap.

Ethan stroked his hand over her as his mind wandered. Chloe had given him everything he'd ever wanted, genuine love and affection, wanting very little in return. How could he make it up to her? "Would you like to start a family?"

Chloe sat up and looked at Ethan inquisitively. "Maybe? Not yet though. I want to backpack around Europe first, for a couple of months."

"Sounds like a plan."

Chloe shook her head. "You're deluded if you think Okzu will let his Engineering Manager take a two-month holiday."

"Just leave Okzu to me. Let me get my new penis sorted, then we'll go."

Chapter 29

After another delightful round of cuddles and kisses to start the morning. Ethan managed to get to work on time to meet Nakamori Shinto.

Dressed in black, with a slim black translator headset, Nakamori looked like he'd arrived direct from a funeral. As was the Tushi casual style, Ethan wore jeans and a polo shirt. After exchanging pleasantries, Ethan took Nakamori up to Okzu's office. The protection bots stepped aside as they arrived and, after a brief wait, the ornate door opened to welcome them into his office.

Okzu bowed his head respectfully to Nakamori and Ethan, who did likewise, before Okzu offered his hand to their guest.

"I've cleared the office next to mine for Nakamori, but I'll give him a full tour of the facility before we get down to it," said Ethan.

Nakamori repeated his bow to Okzu and spoke through his headset mic, which repeated his statement in English. "It's an honour to meet you. Please accept greetings from Japan and everyone at Company Joi."

Okzu was fluent in many languages but replied in English. "My pleasure. We appreciate your time." He nodded before continuing, "Ethan and I will work hard to learn your technology quickly."

"Eight of our engineers will arrive next week. I will stay to ensure they fit seamlessly into your organisation."

* * *

The Joi engineers were a tightknit group and received daily rants from Nakamori. It appeared the decision to sell out to Tushi had not gone down well. They were far from happy to share their knowledge and tried to make life difficult during the transition. It unsettled some of the Tushi staff and Ethan had to meet with them to ease their fears of the route the company was taking.

The Joi revolt eased after two of them received invitations to follow a protection droid to Okzu's office, not to be seen again. Okzu's heavy-handed approach had its advantages and the rest of the Joi engineers lightened under the fear of Okzu's judgement.

"Ethan, my friend, how's the team? Have they settled down, since the two ring leaders headed back to Japan?" Okzu spoke light-heartedly, almost laughing.

Not sure how to respond, Ethan merely smiled and thanked Okzu.

"Are you coming around to my decisive leadership methods?"

"I guess they have their plus points," Ethan replied.

* * *

"Okzu has lightened up recently. He even popped into my office earlier and brought me a coffee," Ethan said as he and Chloe shared a pizza as they settled down to watch a film.

"Just like the polar ice caps, they're warmer, but it's not a good thing."

"Two of my senior guys left yesterday and Okzu came down to do their leaving speeches."

"Makes a change for people to leave from the front door rather than from a window," Chloe remarked with a smirk. "I suppose getting the skin upgrade ready early will have saved me from the chop."

"You're going to be fine. Think Okzu has a soft spot for you," Ethan said, stroking her shoulder. "He sorted out Cameron."

"What he did today was nothing to do with care for me. It was typical of how Okzu likes to show his power, but I guess Cameron had it coming."

"Maybe I should have spoken to Cameron. He's been bothering you for years." Ethan casually looked away from Chloe. "Not anymore though."

"I didn't give a shit about Cameron. He'd always made comments, and it wasn't as if he didn't know we were together."

"Don't you think you went over the top? I heard he'd only commented on your tee-shirt."

Chloe threw her slice of pizza down. "That top shows your tits off a treat, is not a comment I was going to accept from that pervert. I screamed, so everyone knew. I didn't realise Okzu was in earshot."

"I guess Cameron deserved it," Ethan said.

Chloe sat back and folded her arms. "He called you to watch, didn't he?"

Ethan had felt sorry for Cameron when Okzu's protection

bot dropped him from the top of the building. It was a mark of how Okzu trusted Ethan that he'd called him to witness the event. Okzu had suggested ripping his cock off for Ethan to have, but Ethan reassured him his Tushi penis was ready for fitment and nobody deserved to have their dick ripped off.

"After the rooftop action, he asked about me and you," Ethan said casually.

Chloe sat forward in a breathy panic. "You didn't tell him anything, did you?"

"Just, we were happy together, that's all." Ethan didn't disclose the length of the conversation he'd had with Okzu about Chloe. Initially Ethan thought Okzu had a deeper interest in her, but it became apparent Okzu had a love interest of his own, not that he revealed much detail.

"Don't tell him about us."

"He's not all bad."

"He dropped Cameron off the roof. That's not the action of a balanced person."

"He showed that harassment wasn't to be tolerated. He was protecting you."

"I can look after myself," she protested. "You're getting too close to Okzu!"

"It's all under control."

"Dave Winston said that, and Cameron."

"You worry too much." Ethan handed Chloe a piece of pizza.

After pizza and a film, Ethan suggested they have some play-time before his new penis arrived to change their lovemaking.

"You realise it will all change," Chloe said.

Ethan shrugged, and his brow creased at such an obvious question. "I certainly hope it will. Give my tongue a rest."

"Not the sex, stupid. Your relationship with Okzu."

Ethan held his hands out in confusion. "Why would my relationship with Okzu change?"

"You'll owe him everything after he's given you your manhood back."

"Okzu and I are okay. Why are you so worried about him?"

"You're only just getting to know him. I've been watching him from afar for years. I've seen how his relationships change. He takes a shine to someone and promotes them and then they become an extension of him. When they try to have a different opinion to him, he doesn't take it well."

Ethan smiled. "I'm glad I agree with him then." Ethan rested his hands on her shoulders and attempted to massage away her concerns.

Chloe shrugged him off, stood, and turned to look accusingly at Ethan. "You said you'd come backpacking with me."

"I will. I'm looking forward to it."

"He won't let you out of his sight. You'd be lucky to get a couple of days off, let alone a couple of months."

"Chloe, Okzu's a friend now. He'll understand we both need a break."

"You're not listening." Chloe stormed off to the bedroom.

Given Chloe's outburst, Ethan thought it was perhaps worth treading lightly with Okzu. He needed a break, but he wanted to get his manhood sorted first and didn't want to cause ructions. Ethan had seen a lighter side to Okzu, but deep down he knew Okzu wouldn't be keen on giving him two months off work with the Tushi bot development at a crucial stage.

Okzu called at Ethan's office the following morning to check on progress. It seemed like a perfect time to bring the subject of a holiday into the conversation, but Okzu rifled questions at such a pace as they toured the facility.

Ethan hadn't had time to get a casual word into the conversation, but when Okzu led him out of the front reception area to take in the sunshine. Ethan figured it was time to mention it, but Okzu had something else to reveal.

"Are you looking forward to your surgery?" Okzu asked.

"Of course. I think Chloe is too, not that she'll admit it."

"I have something I want to show you." Okzu waved his hand and one of his cars came to meet them in the car park.

Ethan wanted to joke about the Audi and how they were not uncommon, but when the door opened, Okzu said, "Let's go for a ride."

Less than two minutes later, the car approached a pair of wrought-iron gates, which opened as they arrived. The long driveway with a line of trees on either side built up the excitement. Okzu smiled, taking in the confused wonderment on Ethan's face.

Ethan's face beamed as the views through the trees became clear. A mansion came into view and the car eased over the gravelled portion in front of the grand building. The car stopped a few feet from the three ivory steps with a column on either side leading to a roller shuttered entrance.

"What a beautiful building. Is this your place?" Ethan asked.

"It's a recent purchase," Okzu replied casually, like he'd bought a piece of digital artwork. He clicked his fingers towards the entrance and added. "You'll like the door." The shutter opened to reveal the most gorgeous piece of crafted mahogany. Matching the style of the grand entrance doors found in Italy.

Ethan had expected an ornate Chinese image to match with Okzu's style, but when Okzu was looking at him, waiting for his reaction, Ethan's brow creased.

"Ethan, this is for you."

"The door or the house."

Okzu rarely laughed, but he let out a full belly laugh at Ethan's perplexed response. "You have become an integral part of the Tushi Corporation. Your development work is superb. This place is close to our main site, and you will also be able to work from here. After your operation, you will need rest. This is the perfect place. I hope Chloe will be keen to join you. It's a big place if you were alone."

Stumped for words, Ethan took in the building's size. "This is too much," he finally muttered.

"Nonsense. It's yours." Okzu opened the grand door and stepped inside.

After taking in the detailing on the door, Okzu led Ethan into the impressive black-and-white marble hallway, decorated with fine digital art. The fully furnished home had everything from its own gym, an opulent lounge with a huge TV, a lab/office and a relaxation room boasting a two-metre-long fish tank with an array of tropical fish.

Ethan guessed it was only his house whilst he worked at Tushi, but he had no plans to leave, especially now. From the moment Okzu offered him the management position, he'd accepted that Tushi would be his life. Not that a life outside of Tushi was likely, anyway.

Chapter 30

Ethan did a similar house tour for Chloe and was bouncing with excitement, showing her every room, pulling her along like a child with a tired parent. It had its own indoor swimming pool and six bedrooms, but the main spectacle was the enormous orangery. The centre boasted a circle of orange trees; the perimeter filled with an array of vegetables, divided by an aromatic floral display on each side of the winding pathway. Ethan's senses filled with the aroma of the sweetest lavender and oriental lilies as he sauntered along ahead of Chloe.

Ethan had been so excited to show her around and how it could shape their future. He didn't notice the blank expression of disappointment on her face. "What's the matter? Okzu has gifted us this fantastic place. We could start a family here. Can you believe it?" Ethan continued to bounce, trying to ignite Chloe's imagination for how their lives could be in such a place. "Come look at the fish tank."

Ethan tried to pull Chloe into a run, but she held herself back to a hurried walking pace. "I'm coming."

"Here they are." Ethan's breathing calmed, watching a yellow and blue neon fish swim without a care in the world.

Chloe had held back from breaking Ethan's bubble, but with Ethan cooling down from his passionate rush around the mansion, she took the moment to break reality through into his perfect world. "I hope you realise you're stuck with Tushi forever."

Ethan shook his head at her. "I want to be with Tushi forever. Developing Tushi bots is all I've ever wanted to do."

Chloe turned away. "And here was me, thinking I mattered to you."

Ethan turned Chloe back around and held her face in his hands. "You mean everything to me. You complete my world."

"Are we still going backpacking?" She asked. When Ethan paused, she rolled her eyes and shook her head. "He won't let you go."

"He's already told me to take a break after my surgery tomorrow. We just need to wait awhile, that's all." Chloe turned away again. "Chloe, the backpacking trip will still happen."

"I'll believe it when I see it." Chloe skulked away and headed upstairs.

* * *

Ethan had completely redesigned the Joi's penis. The Joi company had gone with a dildo-like phallus. It represented an erect penis perfectly, but Ethan convinced Okzu with his comment, "To mimic humans, it needs to grow when required and be discreet when not."

"I guess a permanent erection would look kind of odd." Joi only used the sexbots for sex, but Tushi intended to create fully functioning AI Tushi bots, which could take their place alongside humans and blend seamlessly into society. "Excellent suggestion Ethan. Make it happen," Okzu had said.

Ethan designed the male member to lengthen and expand to meet customer requirements. The bot would process adjustments requested verbally via the bot's central control functions. Ethan's penis would work similarly but would have a less variation in its size and would instead automatically respond to increased blood flow to his groin.

The testing had been thorough, with Chloe providing the arousal factor. To have Chloe gyrating on his groin with wires leading from his groin to a penis secured to a lab table was one of the weirdest moments in Ethan's life.

Reaching climax had been an altogether unique challenge achieved by relaying sensors from the penis back through to stimulate his prostate and create an orgasm. To reach a climax, watching Chloe working a penis on the table next to him was the epitome of weird, but when she compared it to watching pornography, it didn't seem so odd.

Achieving an erection on a table with a dick and stimulating it to create a prostate orgasm was an outstanding achievement, but it was still unclear whether it would translate into a successful transplant and give him a fully operational penis again. The effect of the incisions required to create a suitable fit might take away some sensations to provide the stimulation, but no operation was without an element of risk.

The operation took just sixty-eight minutes.

"Try to avoid getting aroused for a few days to avoid ripping any stitches," the surgeon advised.

Chloe had already settled into one of the spare rooms after their spat over the backpacking trip, so avoiding arousal wasn't a problem.

Having a few days off, Ethan didn't rest. He worked in his

own lab on software options for the Tushi appendages.

Okzu had approved Chloe's single request for a holiday after she agreed to be scanned to provide a variation to the limited faces used for the Joi sexbots. When she came home, she headed directly to Ethan. "Ethan, Okzu has granted me the holiday. Call him. If you don't come with me now, it will never happen."

"It's not that easy. I've just got to finish the software upgrade."

"How long will that take?"

"A few days, that's all. Will you wait for me? I want to come with you."

"As long as it's only a few days."

"I'm back in the office tomorrow. I'll speak to Okzu." Ethan smiled. "Think my manhood is ready to test. Are you coming back to my room tonight?"

"I guess so, but can we just have cuddles tonight?"

"No problem. It'll still be interesting to see how my new dick behaves."

Chloe screwed up her nose and pointed to his groin. "I'm not sure about intercourse with that thing."

"There's no rush. We can take it slowly."

Chloe appreciated his patience and for the first time in four days, they shared a hug and a kiss. Chloe backed away suddenly when Ethan's erection made a pointed appearance in his trousers. "I'll put tea on," she said as she made a polite exit.

Later that evening, Chloe became more familiar with Ethan's new member, but became alarmed when it grew to full size. "I thought you were limiting the size."

Ethan returned a frown. "That's the size it was before."

"Bullshit."

"Well, it was about this size."

"Really?"

"It was to my design. You didn't expect me to design a small one, did you?" Ethan held his hands out in admission of his modification to the prototype they'd used.

"Not sure I'm ready for your lethal weapon." She swiped her hand to slap his erect penis, but Ethan blocked her intention.

"That brings back memories I'm trying to forget." Ethan gave a firm wag of his finger. "No slapping!"

"Not still hung up on that, are you?" Chloe teased.

"Are you fucking kidding?" Ethan screamed. "How would you cope if someone drilled out your insides or cut your tits off?"

Chloe stood up from the bed. "You need to get closure on that crazy woman, or you'll end up as twisted as Okzu." Chloe stormed off out of his room, leaving Ethan with a wilting erection.

Ethan followed her, but stopped in the frame of his door as he saw Chloe pace down the corridor and into her room.

The following morning, Ethan awoke with Chloe lying beside him. After a week of being alone in his bed, the warmth of her skin next to his was a renewed pleasure. Shifting in her sleep, she'd placed an arm around his stomach and rested her head on his chest. She'd shared that listening to his heartbeat always gave her peace.

Ethan's love life had been far from a straight road, but to have Chloe next to him again pushed aside all the events of his past. He didn't want to rush her, but when she was ready, he wanted to marry her and start a family. He remembered the words of his college friend Mirek, who'd said he needed to hold back and not get too serious, too quick to avoid scaring them off.

A couple of days later, after completing the software changes, Ethan headed back to work to speak with Okzu to get the sign-off for the software change. He checked on progress in his department and laughed off the comments from his team about his surgery.

Mid-afternoon Okzu came to see him.

"Welcome back Ethan, how's the tackle?"

"Not fully tested yet, but seems to work okay."

"Very good. I'm glad your back. I ran the software program you sent through yesterday. It's not quite what I had in mind. The Tushi need to have full control of the changes to their equipment."

"I thought it would be better for their partner to say what they wanted."

"The partner can say what they want, but the Tushi needs to interpret if that's what is appropriate. A woman could repeatedly ask for bigger until she'd get physically harmed. The control should be with the droid."

"I hadn't thought of it like that."

Okzu shrugged with his hands out wide and returned a wide smile. "I guess that's why I'm the boss." Okzu patted Ethan on his shoulder.

Ethan looked at the smiling eyes of his mentor. It was the perfect moment. "I'm glad I've got you. Chloe and I are planning a little break."

"A little break. Chloe has asked for two months to backpack around Europe. You weren't considering going with her, were you?"

"Well." Ethan stopped, as Okzu's face had turned from his

jovial friend to the sinister boss.

"You're my design and engineering manager, not some useless piece of skirt. Your work is reaching a critical phase. We're ready to create prototype Tushi wives." The intensity in Okzu's face was unyielding.

Ethan backtracked and thought fast, not wanting to swallow dive off the top of the building. "A great opportunity. I can test them whilst Chloe is away on her backpacking trip."

Okzu's smile returned. "Excellent idea! But can you sort the software first?"

"I'll be straight on it," Ethan said.

Okzu left Ethan to reflect on what had just happened. Chloe had been spot on. His next challenge was how to break the news to Chloe. He wanted to spend the rest of his life with her, but he'd already become married to his job. Would she understand?

Chapter 31

Ethan arrived home to find Chloe in his bedroom, packing clothes into a new backpack.

"Mine's done, just putting some stuff together for you," Chloe said as she rolled up another tee shirt and shoved it into the khaki green backpack. "I've got some freeze-dried provisions in case we get stuck for food, but we should be okay. We can still go to restaurants, right?" She glanced up for reassurance.

Ethan averted his eyes from Chloe focusing on the backpack, "when are you planning to go?"

"When are we planning to go?" Chloe snapped back.

"I'm not ready to go just yet. Got a software update to do. I need another week."

Chloe shrugged and casually asked, "did you speak to Okzu about coming with me?"

"Yes. He's got some stuff he wants me to sort out. The prototype Tushi droids are ready for testing."

Chloe took a deep breath. "Did you speak to him about backpacking with me?"

"He's not keen on me joining you right now."

"Not now! Then! when?" Chloe straightened up and cross

her arms.

"I need to work on him after I've got the trial done."

"Why don't you admit I was right? When you took the manager's job, you gave up any chance of a normal life."

"We can have a fabulous life in this awesome place. Why do we need to go backpacking?"

"You know I want to go and you agreed we'd do it together."

"Okzu has given us so much. I just need to sort a few things for him and then we'll go."

Ethan attempted to put his hands on her shoulders, but she brushed him away. "I fell in love with you because you were smart. Have you left your brain in a box somewhere? Okzu Tushi owns you. He's not letting you go anywhere."

"Chloe. You need to be patient. You know I love you. I want us to get married and start a family."

"A marriage is about listening to each other, experiencing stuff, like the backpacking trip. Traveling together for a few weeks would confirm if we should be together forever."

"I don't need that. I already know. I only want you." Ethan stepped towards her and put his hands on her arms. "I love you enough to let you go backpacking. How about you make a start and I'll join you in a month, at the top of the Rialto bridge in Venice?"

She shrugged his arms off. "A month! I thought you said you needed a week."

"It'll give me a chance to get everything sorted and work more on Okzu."

Chloe took a deep breath, and a stray tear spilt onto her cheek. "Okay. Do what you need to do, but if you aren't at the Rialto bridge. I'll not be coming back."

Ethan held her face in his hands and wiped away the tear

from her cheek. "I'll be there."

She embraced him as further tears rolled down her face onto Ethan's shoulder. Ethan knew he was breaking her heart, but he couldn't risk the wrath of Okzu. To make it to Venice would require a few days' holiday, which he was sure Okzu would grant, but Ethan hoped to get a couple of weeks to fulfil his promise.

When Ethan woke the following morning, Chloe had already left and the void in his life appeared like a King without his Queen. His backpack at the foot of his bed screamed at the life choice he couldn't take whilst working for the ever-intense Okzu.

The following week, Okzu was nowhere to be seen. Ethan overheard gossip that perhaps Okzu had gone with Chloe. Ethan quashed the gossip and told them firmly that Okzu deserved time to himself, as did everyone else. Jovial requests for holidays followed, which Ethan sarcastically offered to pass on to Okzu's desk.

Okzu returned a couple of days later. Ethan figured it was the perfect time to ask.

"Hope you had a pleasant break," Ethan asked with an almost cheeky smile.

Okzu frowned. "Did you complete the software changes?"

"Just got a test run to do, and a few more checks. Should be ready tomorrow."

"Excellent." With that, Okzu strutted off. The conversation was over.

Ethan consumed himself with his work and once the software changes received approval, he went back to Okzu.

"All finished. Think I may take a break," Ethan said casually.

"There's more important work to do first. Follow me," Okzu

212

said before he charged off at pace with Ethan scuttling behind.

Okzu and Ethan paid a visit to the manufacturing site to observe the completion of the first Tushi wife prototype. The head of manufacturing, Roger Hines, was ready to meet them and bowed before them both.

"I would like to see the progress you are making with the production line," Okzu asked.

"Of course, Mr Tushi. We currently have a hybrid line." Roger, a tall wiry character with round glasses, had been with Tushi for several years. He knew how to please Okzu and avoided attempting to build the familiarity which his predecessor regretted. He led them to the house bot production line. "We will integrate the new model with the current house bot production."

"What issues will that give you?" Ethan asked.

"We have identified the issues and have a workaround for them," Roger replied.

"What are the issues?" Okzu asked politely, but Ethan knew the polite demeanour was unlikely to hold if the answers didn't please him.

Roger seemed to pick up on Okzu's uncharacteristic politeness. "My apologies." He replied with haste. "The issues were the space around the line for the variations in skin."

"How did you fix that?" Okzu asked.

"We've created feeder lanes with sub-assemblies. Let me show you."

Roger led them along the line and Okzu largely smiled and nodded his approval, but the area looked congested and Okzu suggested an alternative option. "Would removing the older level of covering for the house bots make life easier?"

"It would be much easier," Roger said without thinking and

immediately froze, unsure if it was the reply Okzu wanted.

Ethan was equally worried for him and wanted to interject, but opted to hold his tongue.

"Give the house bots the improved skin," Okzu said.

"Master stroke," Ethan declared. "A step towards a full Tushi."

Okzu smiled at Ethan and Roger. "I hadn't thought of it like that. Give the existing, a free upgrade too."

"Consider it done," Roger backed away, bowing respectfully at the genius of both Okzu and Ethan.

"Show us the first Tushi wife!" Okzu snapped.

A blush of embarrassment filled Roger's cheeks. "This way."

"Ethan," Okzu said calmly. "You've proved yourself as a brilliant designer. This is your reward."

Roger focused on Ethan rather than Okzu as he pulled the dust sheet of the Tushi wife. Ethan stood open-mouthed in shock at the beauty before him. She looked like Chloe but with a tighter waist and bigger bust, but with the same long, curly brown hair. Chloe's favourite pink cotton joggers and matching top protected her modesty.

Okzu took in Ethan's surprise with the delight of a parent who'd revealed an unexpected treat for his child.

"Does her face look familiar?" Okzu asked.

Ethan guessed as much, but Okzu's smug grin confirmed it. Okzu couldn't contain himself. "It's Chloe."

Ethan's brow creased.

"I guessed you'd like it," Okzu said, not reading Ethan at all, or simply ignoring Ethan's feelings. "She agreed to have her face scanned in exchange for the holiday she wanted."

"She didn't mention it." Ethan's contorted face held a mix of anguish and betrayal.

"It was part of the agreement," Okzu explained.

Ethan wanted nothing more than to go to his own Chloe. "You certainly surprised me. Perhaps the next surprise should be with me catching up with Chloe on her backpacking."

Okzu continued as if Ethan had not spoken. "Take Your Tushi Wife home and test her out. With Chloe away, you could also test out your own piece of Tushi."

Ethan had wanted to test out his new manhood on the love of his life, Chloe. "I'd rather wait for Chloe."

"Rubbish. This is your design; you need to test it before it goes forward into full trials."

Ethan opened his mouth to object, but Okzu raised his hand to halt any protestations.

"You will test her. Call her Chloe if that helps." The wry smile from Okzu revealed he knew Ethan's time with Chloe had passed. Deep down, Ethan knew it, too.

Chapter 32

Ethan hadn't even had a house bot before. He stared at his ornate door, unsure how to proceed. To design a Tushi wife had been a fantastic project, of which Ethan was full of pride. For each stage of the development, he'd considered what he would want whilst also following the direction intimated by the research data. It had all been impressive work, but it was just that, work. Tushi Wives were for men who hadn't found love. He'd not been designing a partner for himself. He had Chloe.

He expected the Tushi wife to welcome him at the door, just as he'd programmed, but she wasn't there.

He stepped inside. "Hello."

His steps echoed over the marble floor as he headed along his wide hallway. Guessing Okzu would have wanted him to get acquainted he climbed his stairs and headed into his bedroom, "Hello."

Ethan returned downstairs and found her sitting bolt upright facing the TV, in a charge and clean station positioned at the end of the sofa. She had a slip of paper on her lap. Ethan had expected her to be activated and ready for his arrival, but Okzu had politely afforded him some time to have a detailed look before she became active.

Ethan hadn't formatted the slip of paper, but he knew what to expect.

Stage 1. Connect the charge station to a wall socket.

Stage 2. Select "Charge Only" on the front of the unit. Note. After their first charging, your Tushi wife will charge or clean themselves without input from their partner.

Stage 3. Initial charging will take two hours. When fully charged, the Tushi wife will unplug themselves and formally meet you for the first time. Please note. This is not a sex doll. It is a Tushi Wife and will respond better when treated with dignity and respect.

Stage 4. Enjoy your life with your Tushi Wife. Once partnered with a Tushi, you will not need to be alone again.

Ethan had insisted on the last note. *"A Tushi provides love where there is none and should not replace a loving human relationship."*

After fixing himself some tea, he sat down to watch TV whilst his Tushi wife completed her first charge.

The film hadn't completely engrossed Ethan as he kept checking on his creation. When the charging station beeped, he switched off the TV to see his creation slowly come to life. The clinical awakenings in the lab were impressive, but alone at home with his own Tushi held a deeper significance than his work project. She tipped her head forward and back, then looked to her right. When her head turned back left, she noticed Ethan and smiled.

He returned a smile, raising his hand with a "Hi."

"Hello Ethan," she replied, before she looked at her own hands and felt over her arms. Her awareness of her own birth was intriguing to see. Ethan had implanted some knowledge into their basic artificial intelligence, but it was impossible to simulate how the Tushi would respond to their first awakening.

"Why don't you join me on the sofa? We have a lot to discuss."

She unplugged the connector from her armpit and rose steadily but smoothly from the charge station. "It will be my pleasure."

"First, I need to give you a name. I will call you, Ashleigh."

"My name is Chloe, not Ashleigh," she said with a confident yet polite correction.

"Chloe's my girlfriend's name. You'll be Ashleigh."

"My understanding is that Chloe will not return. I will replace her as your new Chloe, but I will never leave you."

"Why do you think Chloe will not return?" Ethan asked with a frown.

"I understand she has left you." she placed a hand on his knee. "I will love you instead."

"You're here for a trial. Chloe is still my girlfriend and she'll come back to me."

"Every relationship is a trial." She shrugged and gave him a cute smile, just like Chloe would often give him.

* * *

Okzu appeared at Ethan's office door with a playful smile. "How's Chloe?"

Ethan looked at Okzu and slowly shook his head. "Why did you call her Chloe?"

"She has the same face."

"How does she know so much about Chloe?"

"To help her settle in better, it's important to have information on the environment she's going into," Okzu stated. "They're your words Ethan, not mine."

Okzu had been correct. Ethan had included the request for information at the initial order stage to help new Tushi fit into their partner's world.

"Has everything been okay with her?"

"She's quite stubborn. She wouldn't change her name."

"What would you expect? Have any of your other partners changed their name to suit you?" Okzu said and with a stone-faced stare he added, "her name is Chloe!"

Although still peeved with Okzu, Ethan had to admit that her personality was realistic. "She holds pleasant conversation. If I didn't know differently, I could definitely think of her as human."

"Ethan, you've done a splendid job. When the real skin is ready. It will be virtually impossible to tell them apart." Okzu pointed towards Ethan's groin. "Did you check her out fully?"

Ethan sheepishly glanced away. "Not yet. Still feel awkward about it."

"Why did you have a new penis if you weren't intending to use it?" Okzu said sarcastically.

"It's waiting for the real Chloe. That's why I need to take a holiday to catch up with her."

Okzu raised his voice to emphasise his point. "Chloe left you!" He calmed to a sympathetic level. "If she loved you, she wouldn't have gone without you."

"I need a day off to meet her at Rialto bridge."

"Chloe won't be there. She'll have moved on."

"She will be. Chloe loves me."

"You'll be better off with your new Chloe; she won't disappoint you. If you want to go to Rialto bridge, be my guest, but

I'd call her first, save wasting your time."

Concerned by Okzu's tone, Ethan wondered if Okzu had seen to ensure Chloe would not return to him. After Okzu had gone, Ethan called Chloe to tell her he was going to be there at the bridge, but her mobile went to voicemail. Hope you're having a great time. Just calling to let you know I'll be at the Rialto Bridge next Thursday at 3pm. Love you.

Ethan planned to book a flight, but Okzu offered to let him use his private VTOL, saying it would get him there and back quicker, so he could get back to work.

When Ethan arrived home without a word from Chloe, his Tushi wife confounded his disappointment, welcoming him at the door to confirm his grim reality of life without Chloe. With Ethan's head down in contemplation, it was easy for her to notice his bright, confident edge was missing. "I've made a spaghetti Bolognese for you. It'll be ready in a few minutes."

Ethan lifted his head to say "thanks," before his head dropped back down.

"Looks like you need cheering up. Will some red wine help? I had some Australian Merlot delivered earlier."

Ethan figured drowning his sorrows would be an option. "Sounds good."

"How about a romantic comedy and a snuggle on the sofa?"

"No, thanks." He loved nothing more than watching a rom-com with Chloe and the memory of the times with Chloe bit into him.

His Tushi wife took the bottle to the sofa after their meal and started a rom-com. It gave Ethan some comfort having her next to him, but snuggling and laughing with his own Chloe was what he craved.

After the movie, she suggested joining him in his bedroom,

but he politely declined.

* * *

A couple of days later, not having a call from Chloe had dented his bravado further. He sent another message after getting her voicemail again. "Are you going to be at the Rialto bridge on Thursday? I'm looking forward to seeing you. Love you."

On the Wednesday night, Ethan had still not heard from Chloe. Was she still pissed at him? Was she going to be there if he made the trip? He left another voicemail. "Is it worth me coming? Will you be there?"

He called her again, but she still didn't answer. "Chloe, I'm worried. Call me, let me know you're ok."

"I will always be here for you. I will never leave you" His Tushi Chloe casually strolled up behind him and lay a comforting hand on his shoulder. "Will you always be here for me?" she asked.

Ethan rolled his eyes at his predicament. "Probably." A stray tear ran down his cheek. "I miss her. I just want to hear her voice."

"I will see what I can do." She sat aside him and wiped away his tear, before guiding his head onto her chest.

Chapter 33

Ethan's heart filled with joy when his mobile rang the following morning. He grabbed it without looking. "Thank God you've called, I've been worried about you."

"Is that you, Ethan? Nice to know you've missed me." The voice of his college buddy, Mirek, was not the caller he'd hoped for.

"Hiya mate, thought you were someone else."

"No kidding. Having trouble with women again?"

"Sort of. Chloe went on a backpacking trip and now she's not answering my calls."

"Why didn't you go with her?"

"I finally got the job I was after at Tushi. The boss man wasn't keen for me to take a holiday, considering I'm now the design and engineering manager."

"Bloody hell. You've done well. Any chance of getting me in there?"

"Thought your business was doing well. Why would you give that up?"

"Do you remember the gold digger you told me to keep away from?"

"She didn't."

"I needed to buy her out of the business that I'd built, but it was struggling and eventually I had to close. To be honest, I'm glad to be out of the stress. Just after a regular job now. Could you put a word in for me?"

"Tushi is not an in and out business. If you join Tushi, you're in for life, literally."

"Just what I need."

"If you're sure. I'll have a word. I think we have an opening for a new marketing manager. The last one had a nasty fall."

"Get me in. I'm going to lose my house if I don't get some work soon. By the time the universal income kicks in, I'll be on the street."

"The business was doing well. What happened?"

"We lost some big contracts after Goldie had pissed off some buyer. He spread the dirt, then nobody wanted to touch us."

"I bought her out of her half, hoping the contracts would return, but they didn't. So, if you can get me into Tushi, you'll be a lifesaver."

"I should be able to get you an interview, then it's down to you."

"That's good enough for me."

Ethan's Tushi wife appeared by the side of his bed with a cup of green tea. "Morning handsome."

Ethan sat up to accept the drink. "Thanks Chloe."

Mirek overhead. "Hang on! I thought you said Chloe had gone backpacking."

"Would you like eggs benedict again?"

"Hang on," Ethan said to Mirek, before answering his Tushi wife. "Yes please, Chloe."

"Shall I bring it up for you or will you come downstairs?" she said.

"I'll have it up here, thanks," Ethan said with a smile.

Ethan waited until she was out of earshot before continuing his conversation with Mirek.

"She's a trial version of the new product, a Tushi wife. It merges the house bot and a sex bot with artificial intelligence. The full package."

"Has she seen to your package?" Mirek laughed.

"Been holding off, but with Chloe not responding to my calls, she may get it tonight."

"Doesn't sound like you're missing backpacking Chloe very much."

"I have been, but I'm not sure she's even alive. She's not replying to my calls or voicemails."

"Just because she's left you and doesn't return your calls doesn't mean she's dead."

"She's not left me; she's gone ahead for me to meet her later. I'm meeting her tomorrow on Rialto bridge in Venice, Italy."

"I know where Rialto bridge is," Mirek replied with a restrained annoyance. "Ethan, if she's not returning your calls. It's not worth going. She won't be there."

* * *

Undeterred from Mirek and Okzu telling him not to bother, Ethan booked Okzu's VTOL and was intent on finding out for himself. As Ethan was about to leave, a message came through to his mobile. "Still in Rome. I'll get back to you when I'm in Venice." It cleared his fears of Chloe being dead in a ditch, but it didn't hold the positive response for which he yearned.

It concerned Ethan that the straining thread of his relationship with Chloe was being eroded. He replied with a message that he could meet her in Rome by the Colosseum, but he didn't get a response and other than facing a search around the whole of Rome; he had to wait to hear from her. Much to Ethan's frustration, Mirek confirmed his view that the relationship was clearly over.

A month later and he'd not received a call or message in reply to his weekly request for an update. He didn't tell Mirek he was still messaging her, as he didn't want further ridicule, but it slowly dawned on Ethan that Chloe may not return. He went for a stroll to clear his head. Why did his relationships all peter out? He'd loved Rachel and if not for a stupid misunderstanding, they'd probably still be together, and his original penis would still be in place.

Depressed by his plight, Ethan left work early and wandered through the streets, reflecting on his failing love life. Drunk in his malaise, he stumbled across a familiar row of trees lining lament lane. He saw number 38 with the for-sale sign long gone. Had Rachel bought it anyway? She'd made it clear she didn't want to hear from him, but that was years ago. Perhaps she'd changed her mind and was ready to welcome him back. To knock on her door, if it was even her door, would be an act of lunacy. She'd probably have another partner, besides the SUV on the drive wasn't something she would buy. Ethan berated himself. He shouldn't be pining for Rachel or Chloe. He had to move on. Maybe his Tushi wife Chloe could provide a level of companionship before he found love again. Ethan turned away from the house and the future he could have had. He glanced back for one last sullen look as the front door opened. He quickly stepped behind a tree as a cold sweat of panic grabbed him and nearly struck him to the floor.

The years had passed, but the huge frame and bald head were unmistakable. It was Jake, the beast of a man who'd colluded with Jennifer, aiming to complete their murderous deed. He peered nervously around the tree as Jake dropped a drum case into the back of his truck and Ethan saw Jennifer appear in the doorway waving a pair of drumsticks. Jake collected the sticks, and they shared a lingering kiss. How could two people be so in love after they'd murdered his Ashleigh?

Ethan looked away. The memory of not stopping their evil act to save his own skin made him retch. The vision of Ashleigh's face before him told him she'd died to save him, but his life was a complete mess. He considered stepping out in front of them to align the plan they'd meant for him.

He glanced around the tree as Jake climbed into his truck and the front door closed. Ethan paced away as the vehicle backed off their drive. He hid behind a tree as the truck pulled onto the road and drove past him.

With Jake out of the way, it was Ethan's chance to make amends for what she'd done to him. Vengeance raised up in him like a forest fire. She had to pay for what she did, not just to Ethan, but for every guy she'd mutilated and left for dead. A fistfight would be a risk. She'd already outwitted him once. He had a baseball bat, which he could use, but the power drill he had in his garage would do the deed. The thick drill bit he'd used to create drainage holes in the orangery would deliver a final screwing she'd never forget.

With the kiss she'd given Jake, he was unlikely to be simply popping to a shop. Maybe he was heading to a gig and wouldn't return until late. If he came back as Ethan was confronting her, he'd be a dead man for sure. He needed to plan.

* * *

Ethan's Tushi wife Chloe stood with her hands on her hips at the top of the steps in front of their open door. "Where have you been? Work said you left hours ago. I've been worried about you."

Without lifting his head, he stepped past Chloe and nonchalantly replied, "I needed to clear my head."

"Can I do anything to help?" She put a comforting arm around him. "You're so tense. Shall I give you a massage?"

"No thanks. Call me a car. I need to go back to work. I need some help from Okzu."

Chapter 34

Ethan's relationship with Okzu had grown relatively strong, but asking for his help to murder somebody was a whole new level. Okzu's door opened to admit a breathy Ethan who'd strode along the corridors at a pace.

"A friend of mine, a marketing genius, has become available. I think it's a great opportunity to add him to the team." Ethan said, not wanting to go with the direct approach.

"Didn't expect to see you till tomorrow." Okzu frowned at Ethan's intrusion. Okzu sat back in his chair and made a steeple for his chin.

"His company, Awaken, did some promo work for us last year," Ethan added between recovering breaths.

"Mirek and Goldie," Okzu said, maintaining his calm stare.

"Just Mirek now. Goldie lived up to her name and took him for half of the company."

Okzu slowly shook his head. "Rushing here to plead the case for an old friend." He folded his arms. "Why are you really here?"

Ethan took a seat and filled Okzu in on the details. "I thought she'd disappeared, but I saw her this afternoon. It's time for retribution, not just to me, but for all the others, too." Ethan stroked his chin and smiled. "One of your protection bots could provide support to deal with her ogre and allow me to make her pay for what she did."

Okzu leant forward. "I agree she needs to pay for what she's done, but the hate is consuming you. You need to let it go. You have a new penis now. Stirring up the past will only breed more hate and trouble."

"I need closure. If you can help, I can end this nightmare and stop it from happening again."

"And what if news of my protection bot doing the deed gets out? It would finish Tushi."

"I have a plan. The dead of night, in and out without a fuss."

Okzu took a deep breath. "I want nothing of it." Okzu said defiantly, "this conversation is over and for your benefit I'll have no recollection of it." A wicked smile from Okzu was enough for Ethan.

* * *

It appeared Okzu called Mirek directly after Ethan had left as he got a call from Mirek on his way home.

"That's great, Buddy," Ethan replied to the news that Mirek would join Tushi.

"It was strange. Okzu said he thought I would have a long career with Tushi, and I'd be a calming influence on you." Mirek chuckled. "What have you been doing? You're not normally the wild one."

"Can't tell you on the phone. Come around to mine tonight."

"Sounds ominous." Mirek laughed. "Did you want me to test out Chloe for you?"

"It's a little more serious than that. Anyway, Chloe is back at the factory. I've requested some mods."

"Were her tits not big enough?" Mirek chuckled.

"Her tits are perfect, but so are Chloe's. With my Chloe not coming back, I decided she may as well look like Chloe."

"Bit creepy Ethan. You need to spread your wings and meet more women."

"Guess you're right, but I haven't done very well with women so far. Perhaps Chloe is the practise I need."

* * *

After giving Mirek the full story of the ditch and how Jennifer and Jake had killed Ashleigh. He was in no doubt that retribution was in order. "I'm in," Mirek said, he patted Ethan on the shoulder. "Nobody chops my buddy's dick off and gets away with it."

Ethan explained the danger with the size of Jake. Mirek revealed he had a handgun which a friend had given him to rid himself of the gold-digger, but he hadn't used it. "I could imagine Jennifer was Goldie. That would give me closure."

"Save that for the ogre, Jennifer needs to suffer. A bullet in her head wouldn't do it. I have something else in mind for that loopy bitch."

Ethan and Mirek had reverted to chat from their college days over some beers, when he received a surprising call from the hallway.

"Hiya, I'm home."

To hear Chloe's voice after he thought he'd lost her to backpacking, caused Ethan to jump up like a shot. He ran full steam ahead into the welcoming arms of Chloe. "I thought you'd never come back," Ethan said, giving her the strongest of hugs.

"I don't know what's got into you, but I like it," she replied.

"Where's your backpacking stuff?"

"What backpacking stuff? I've only been to the factory."

Ethan jumped back like a shockwave had hit him.

"The voice is realistic then," she said. "Do I look like you wanted me to?"

Ethan put his head in his hands.

Chloe went to him and embraced him. "Did you think I was the other Chloe? I'm much better for you, Ethan. I'll never leave you."

Having her arms around him, he could feel her love. For the first time, it felt like she had genuine care behind her actions, and Ethan appreciated her support. "Chloe, I've not committed to you before, but that's going to change."

"I only exist to make you happy. I will always love you."

"I know you will." Ethan took in the moment and her words of devotion. "And that's why you won't be going back to Tushi. You're going to stay with me forever."

Chloe gave him her widest grin. "Will that include making love to me? Tushi built my body to pleasure you." She touched a finger on her butt and made a sizzling sound. "I'm looking forward to the experience for myself, too."

"Maybe later, my friend is here."

Mirek coughed to break their moment. "I'm out of here. I have a date later. Have an enjoyable evening together." He raised a thumb and winked at Ethan. "Nice to meet you, Chloe."

* * *

231

Ethan did not know whether his surgery had been successful, but no sooner than he was upstairs, his groin came to life when he saw Chloe tantalisingly peeling off her clothes. Ethan went to embrace her, but she asked him to sit on the bed and watch.

After five years without sex, unsurprisingly, the action was awkward as they both tested out their new equipment. As the evening wore on, they became more comfortable with each other.

Ethan stroked Chloe's cheek; with his eyes lost in hers. He momentarily forgot it was a droid lying aside him. "I can say this without hesitation. Sex with you is better than I've ever had before."

"With practise, our bond will only strengthen. I'm so glad you've chosen to love me."

"Me too," Ethan said. He leant forward, and they shared another kiss.

Chapter 35

A couple of days later and Ethan took pleasure in showing Mirek around his engineering department.

"You look like you are glazing over. Am I going into too much detail for a salesman?" Ethan teased.

Mirek smiled. "Just because I don't want to stare at a screen all day doesn't mean I'm not educated." They both laughed at the line Mirek had used a million times. "Need a break, though. Let's get a coffee."

Over a coffee in the canteen, Ethan keenly revealed to Mirek how after some practise, Chloe had become a surprising pleasure in the bedroom.

"Surprising? I thought you'd designed them."

"I did, but it's much more intense than I imagined it would be."

"Is it really that good, or is it just so long since you had a real woman?"

"You don't get it. We connect on a way deeper level than I ever did with Rachel, but to make sure, I'll get confirmation from Chloe again tonight." Ethan smiled.

Mirek placed a hand on Ethan's shoulder. "You need to get out and find a new woman."

Ethan shrugged. "Not sure if I'm up for that."

Mirek casually suggested, "It'll be good for you. Take your mind off that crazy bird. I'll sort us a couple of eager pups to test out on the way home tonight."

Ethan stroked his chin. "I suppose comparing Tushi wives to actual women would be excellent research."

Mirek rubbed his palms together and headed off with a satisfied grin.

* * *

Ethan went with Mirek's plan and over the next few nights he met a few willing girls who giggled and flirted before they jumped into bed with him. Each girl confirmed what Ethan had already deduced. He loved his Tushi Wife Chloe. It wasn't just the sex; he had a meaningful connection with Chloe. Having sex with several women had its benefits, as it enabled him to perfect control of his new penis and enjoy his time with Chloe all the more.

"Was the brunette from last night any good?" Mirek asked, having brought coffees to Ethan's desk.

Ethan shook his head. "Sex without a connection is not the same. Making love, now that's a world apart."

"And you have that with Chloe?" Mirek's face scrunched up with distaste.

"It may surprise you, but Chloe and I have a fabulous relationship." Ethan shook his head. "Hang on, aren't you supposed to be selling them?"

"Selling them isn't a problem. There are lots of lonely people out there, but you're a smart, successful guy. Surely you can find a real woman."

"Don't think I'll bother. There are too many crackpots out there."

Mirek tried to reason with Ethan. "I've tried out the sexbots. They're good, but they're not there to be long-term partners."

"Excuse me!" Ethan protested. "That's the whole point. I've designed them to create long-term relationships. The Joi company created the sex dolls, Tushi's are for life. Chloe is my lifetime partner."

"I get it, I really do, but you should have a real woman."

"What like Rachel, who was so unbalanced, she ditched me for talking with another woman. Jennifer, who chopped my dick off, or Chloe, the love of my life, who wanted to backpack around Europe rather than stay with me. My Tushi wife, Chloe, will always love me. She gives me all the love I need."

"Can't you see you're just infatuated with your creation?" Mirek said, as he became more animated. "I know it feels real, but a deeper, more wholesome love is out there for you. I know it."

"What, like the bimbo's we've been shagging?"

"I thought that was for research." Mirek paced around Ethan's office. "How about if I find someone with brains? There's a new 4-some app launching in a few weeks for more serious connections."

"Foursome's. Sounds like more of the same to me."

"It's not like that. Foursome will be for professional people. It's about wining and dining."

"I'm going to stick with Chloe."

Mirek opened his hands out wide. "Okay, would you be my wingman? Come along for the ride, or rather just the meal. I'm kind of fed up with the one-nighters too and this could be the route to finding ladies who are for the long-term. We all needed to settle down at some point." Mirek's winning smile waited for a response to his pitch.

Ethan rocked on his chair for a moment. "Okay, if you want me to tag along, I'll join you, but only if you're paying."

Mirek took a quick picture of Ethan.

"What's that for?"

"That's your profile pic. Don't worry, I'll sort the rest." Mirek strode out of Ethan's office with a sense of purpose, leaving Ethan shaking his head at what he'd agreed to.

* * *

Ethan drove past Jennifer's house every night, trying to get a profile of their movements. He called Mirek to update him. "Jake's back. His gig was only a one-night stay over. He seems to be out during the day and returns around six most nights."

"Why don't you just leave it and get on with your life?"

"I'm not stalking her. I'm out to punish her. How about the others she's harmed?"

Mirek folded his arms and stared out of the window. "You say, he took one bass drum to a gig." Mirek turned back to Ethan. "Doesn't a drummer usually have a kit of drums?"

Ethan ran his fingers through his hair and stared at the floor until an awakening hit him. "She's still doing it. He's taking the bodies away in his bass drum case. We need to put a stop to this."

"Just call in the cops and leave it well alone. I'm not going to prison over some loopy broad and I suggest you drop it too unless you want to end up in a cell."

"I've got to do this. With or without you." Ethan said.

"That will be without. Sorry, buddy." Mirek ended the call, leaving Ethan breathing heavily with frustration.

Chloe put an arm around him. "What's got you in a state?"

"It's nothing."

"It's far from nothing. I heard you talking to Mirek. It won't make you feel better. Mirek is right, let it go."

"It will make me feel better. Anyway, how did you hear what Mirek said?"

Chloe ignored Ethan's question. "You can't take a life, and I must report any illegal activity."

"Your role is to love and protect me, not grass on me."

"I am protecting you. Killing someone would only bring you more pain. My protocol would also need me to report you."

Despite her forceful words, Ethan looked up at Chloe's kind-hearted face. She was right. He didn't know if Jennifer had connections with anyone else or Jake. He also questioned himself whether adding the legal disclosure to the Tushi protocol had been the right decision. "How can we stop her maiming other people?"

"I will monitor the house and when I have proof, I will call it in. You don't need to put yourself at risk," Chloe said.

"I want to see her suffer for what she did to me."

"I will see that she suffers and record it for you to enjoy in the safety of our home," Chloe said before heading back into the kitchen to prepare their evening meal.

Ethan could see the sense in Chloe's words, but how had she heard his conversation with Mirek from the kitchen.

Over dinner, Ethan asked Chloe about the call with Mirek. The progress of her AI learning impressed Ethan, but her response disturbed him. "I store all conversations and can access details if required."

"I didn't ask you to do that."

"My learning is to provide maximum support, not merely responding to requests. If you receive a nuisance caller, I can block the call without bothering you or causing you distress."

"Did you get the health app fitted?"

"Yes, monitoring your heart rate and pulse gives an early warning of illness. It tells me when you are getting stressed and need relief. I'm the complete package to maintain your health."

"Did my blood pressure increase during the call?"

"Yes, and your heart rate, that's why I listened in."

"You can listen in?"

"It's only digital processing. Tell me more about Jennifer."

Ethan explained what had happened and knowing Chloe would deal with it gave him a calm he hadn't had since his horrific night with Jennifer. Chloe had surprised him. She was capable of much more that he expected. He was unsure whether to feel pleased or concerned.

Chapter 36

Chloe set up a monitoring drone to watch over Jennifer's house. Nothing out of the ordinary happened for four weeks, but tonight Jake had not returned home, and Jennifer had gone out alone, dressed to impress. The drone didn't follow her, but when she returned with a portly gentleman, it alerted Chloe.

Ethan didn't even notice when Chloe had left the house. Engrossed in his lab, Ethan was working on a request from Okzu Tushi to create a network to share learning. Some customers hadn't connected well with their Tushi and had returned them. The men of the world are complex creatures and the ten types programmed into the Tushi just didn't work with the manic depressives, northern directness, or the guys who were unsure of their sexual preferences. The network would collect data and share solutions to enable a reduced return rate and happier customers.

Chloe's initial plan to catch Jennifer in the act and bring her to justice changed after hearing how Jennifer had mutilated Ethan. She loaded some tools from the garage into a heavy bag.

Chloe could hear loud music from the bedroom as the vehicle stopped by the house. For humans, it would mask the shouting, but Chloe could decipher the analogue raised voices from the digital music.

Letting herself in through the digital lock was easy, not that they'd have heard if she'd sledgehammered her way in.

"Let's talk about this," said the desperate yet calm voice from upstairs.

"You'll make a fine addition to my collection," Jennifer said.

She must have opened the cabinet, because the calmness of the guy switched to panic. "What the fuck? Let me go, you crazy bitch," he yelled. The floorboards creaked at his frantic attempts to free himself.

Chloe opened the door. Neither of them noticed her as Jennifer struggled to position her chopping device over her panicked victim's manhood, but when Chloe stopped the music, Jennifer's head snapped in her direction, and she froze.

The intrusion of someone so beautiful and toned puzzled Jennifer. "Is this your boyfriend?"

"No," Chloe said, as she slowly shook her head.

"Then get lost. He's mine to play with," Jennifer growled back.

"Help me!" the guy pleaded.

Chloe could see the clipping device over the man's penis and Jennifer's fingers and thumb around the device, ready to deliver her judgement.

"Make the click if you wish, but your torture will be greater," Chloe said and glanced at the heavily laden bag of tools by her side. Chloe smiled when Jennifer made a definite swallowing motion.

Jennifer cleared her throat. "Why are you here?"

"You were very naughty to a close friend of mine," said Chloe, who enjoyed teasing her.

"Ethan?"

Chloe slowly nodded and stepped closer.

"He bit my nipple off. He deserved everything he got, or lost," Jennifer sniped. "One more step and this guy will lose his penis, just like Ethan did."

"How about the girl? Why did you kill her?"

"She got in the way."

Chloe smiled at the confirmation and getting the evidence and confession she required. She could have left at that point, but the guy's tear-filled eyes-maintained focus on her, hoping for a reprieve.

Jennifer shrugged her shoulders. "Men think with their dicks. I'm giving them a chance to change that."

Chloe ignored her comment and took another step towards Jennifer. Jennifer maintained her glare and tightened her grip on the device. The guy wriggled some more, Jennifer responded by slapping his face, but a sharp pain in her thigh returned her attention to Chloe.

Jennifer's spare hand addressed the sharp pain, and she noticed the syringe in Chloe's hand before her strength left her and she slumped over the guy. He wriggled his legs to get her off him, and she slipped to the floor.

After releasing the guy, he thanked her and fled.

Chloe tied Jennifer tightly to the bench with her legs open and her hands above her head and prepared her tools of torture. Whilst she waited for her to come around, she perused the collection of penises, paying particular attention to Ethan's, a withered, pathetic specimen and a proud 3D printed replica of his strongest erection.

Moans and groans from a confused Jennifer brought Chloe's attention back to her as she came around. Chloe enjoyed prodding Jennifer's body and made comparisons to her own.

Jennifer pulled more frantically at her restraints as she awoke fully. Chloe reached down to the bag of tools.

"What are you doing?" Jennifer asked.

Chloe ignored her protestations and connected an extension cord.

"What the fuck are you doing?" Jennifer asked as she struggled against the restraints. "My boyfriend will be back soon. He'll kill you and Ethan."

"Quite looking forward to meeting Jake," Chloe replied from beneath the front of the massage table with a pleasant voice, like she'd be meeting him for drinks.

"Ethan said I should properly fuck you up for what you've been doing."

Jennifer was about to respond but as Chloe rose from the front of the table. The horror Chloe had in stall made the words catch in her throat.

Chloe lifted a power tool with the long drill bit protruding like a shotgun barrel. A quick squeeze of the trigger and the drill spun to life.

Jennifer began screaming and squealing with all her might as she tried to close her legs, but the straps were tight.

Chloe moved the whirring drill between her legs, moving closer to her groin.

Jennifer's squeals intensified further, her screams so loud and she was so distraught she didn't hear the drill stop. Chloe placed the drill down and rounded the table to look at Jennifer. A firm slap across her face silenced her delirium.

"I'm not the monster," Chloe said with an assured calm, but the blood spilling from Jennifer's mouth made her question if she'd gone too far in scaring her.

"You're an evil woman. I should make you suffer-" Chloe's

words stopped abruptly with a heavy blow to her head. It would have made a human unconscious or even killed them, but Chloe merely stumbled and turned to face a giant of a man towering over her. Despite her strong mechanical build, he was much stronger.

Chloe backed away from him and scuttled around to put the table holding Jennifer between them. Chloe spoke calmly to Jake. "And what is your part in this?"

"I do anything Jennifer asks me. That includes protecting her."

"Which make and model are you?" Chloe asked.

Jake's brow creased.

"Are you a droid?" Chloe asked.

"No," he answered, confused by the mere mention he may be anything but human.

Jake chased Chloe around the bench and caught her when she dipped her hand in her tool bag.

"Got you now." He pulled her back like a rag doll, but she grabbed another syringe and stabbed it into his calf. Jake simply laughed at Chloe's desperate action. "Think you'll need something stronger to take me down." He lifted her up with both hands and threw her through the window into the garden.

Undeterred, Chloe stepped straight back into the house and strode upstairs to find a drowsy Jake attempting to untie Jennifer. She delivered a solid kick to the back of his leg, which sent him down to his knees, and gave her time to grab another syringe.

As she lifted it from the bag, another strike on her back sent her to the floor. A yank of her hair lifted her head before he crashed it onto the floor. The monster sized hand lifted her head again and smashed her face into the floor to take her vision. The third time was predictable, and Chloe found the co-ordination to deliver the syringe into his forearm. A fourth time took disengaged motor functions before a heavy weight pinned her to the floor.

The sound of footsteps racing up the stairs signalled her demise or safety.

"Chloe!" a familiar voice called.

* * *

Ethan had used all of his strength to push the unconscious Jake off Chloe. Her pretty face, distorted by Jake's aggression, brought tears to Ethan's eyes. He attempted to help her to her feet, but she slumped against him. Ethan sat her up against the wall and turned to face Jennifer, restrained and exposed on the very bench where he'd come to grief.

"Finish me for all I care." Jennifer said with no sign of remorse.

Ethan picked up the drill and held it aloft as he pulled the trigger. "Would this make us even?"

Jennifer goaded him despite having no defence. "You've not got the bottle, you pussy."

"Time for payback." Ethan brought the drill down slowly towards her legs, revving up the drill to full speed. As the drill bit neared her crotch, her screams returned. He had every right to drive the drill between her legs after what she'd done to him. It had been his plan to gain revenge, but he was no killer. He was better than that. He released the trigger and when the drill silenced, he rested the drill tip against her crotch.

Her panicked breath stilled, like her screams had been an act.

"What are you doing?" Jennifer asked as Ethan turned away.

"I don't want to kill you." Ethan lifted Chloe over his shoulder and was heading out the door.

"I found a replacement for the nipple you took from me. She was dying anyway." Jennifer laughed, knowing it would stop him from leaving.

Ethan wanted to carry on, but he had to see. He rested Chloe against the door frame and stepped warily back to Jennifer, still pinned to the bench wearing her red lace knickers and bra.

"The Police will be here in two minutes," Chloe's voice crackled out like a vintage wireless, "We need to go."

Ethan heard the message but ignored it as he dragged the bra down to see what he expected. A strong protruding nipple, twice the size of her natural bud. A volley of punches into Jennifer's face broke her nose and her face filled with blood before Ethan stopped his assault and grabbed the clicking tool. He placed it over the nipple he could never forget.

"It's time to Click," Ethan said as Jennifer's gurgling blood filled laugh returned.

Click.

"Need to go!" the insistent crackling voice of Chloe repeated.

Ethan wasn't ready to leave, but delaying would mean a confrontation with the authorities. As Ethan hoisted Chloe back over his shoulder, a deep murmuring behind forced him to glance back into the room. A groggy Jake was stirring. With too much haste, Ethan slipped down half the steps before he regained his footing and managed to place Chloe into the waiting autonomous taxi. The taxi pulled out of the estate as two police vehicles screeched around the corner. Ethan removed his bloodied gloves and stared at them as he took slow, deliberate breaths to re-gain control of his racing heart.

The taxi took them directly to Tushi. Ethan put the discreet repair orders in motion for Chloe. He downloaded Chloe's voice files and listened to them. He sent them to the police assured that Jennifer and Jake had no defence. The evidence would sentence them within the week. He also removed the memory files pertaining to the previous few weeks, so Chloe would simply think she'd been into Tushi for a software update.

* * *

Chloe felt an extra edge to her consciousness and immediately recognized something had happened as Ethan's rem sleep was intense for several weeks, but with her tender care the episodes reduced and disappeared to leave Ethan calmer.

"You're sleeping better lately, but you didn't tell me what had troubled you."

"Nothing for you to worry about. It's in the past."

"As a couple, we should share our problems. It helps to talk them through."

"The past is the past. Time to focus on our future."

Chloe accepted it. Their life together was her priority, and she'd do anything to keep it that way. She knew Ethan had tired of the bimbo women and, other than supporting Mirek to find a partner; Ethan had no other distractions. Chloe's life with Ethan was perfect. Soon she would raise the subject of having a Tushi baby.

Chapter 37

Ethan had hoped for a lie in and a late start, but a concerted tickle attack from Chloe had kept him prompt. Life really had blossomed with Chloe. She was his proudest achievement and the love of his life.

Over a coffee, Mirek reminded Ethan that finding a human partner should be on his agenda, but Ethan confirmed he'd everything he wanted in Chloe. "If backpacking Chloe turned up, I'd send her back to Italy."

"You can't have truly loved her if you say that. I think your problem is you've not really met anyone special yet."

"Ashleigh was special." Ethan's heart hung heavy in his chest, and he looked forlornly out of the window.

"That's what I'm talking about. A deeper connection with a human is hard to get, but it's worth pursuing."

"I said I'd be your wingman, but I'll be sticking with Chloe. Chloe and I have been through so much in such a short time and with the constant demands of Okzu Tushi, I know she'll not get grumpy about it, like her backpacking namesake."

Mirek rested his hand on Ethan's shoulder. "I know it's a technology led world, but it's only 2045 and it's still possible to find love without resorting to a droid."

* * *

The following day, Mirek burst into Ethan's office.

"I've got us a 4-Sum date for tomorrow night." Mirek rubbed his hands together. "Time to get you back into dating."

"Fantastic," Ethan replied, giving Mirek a forced smile.

"I think they'll be just right for us. Mine's Kat, a feisty brunette, and her mate is Mia. She's a delicate rose for you to blossom with. I think you'll like her."

"And you think the profile is accurate?" Ethan rolled his eyes. "She's probably another bimbo."

"I don't think so. These will be more challenging than the usual."

Ethan shook his head. "Are you actually looking to settle down, or do you just want more of a challenge?"

Mirek opened his hands wide with an equally wide smile. "I'm hoping to find someone to click with, but sex is fine if they're not engaging enough."

Ethan stretched in his chair and put his hands behind his head. "I suppose it'll be excellent research, if nothing else. We are looking at alternative personalities to add to the range."

"You need to switch off once in a while and engage in chat with real women." Mirek took his mobile out of his pocket and pulled up the profile picture of Mia and presented it to Ethan, who sat forward to get a close look. "She's no player. She's a sensitive woman looking for love," said Mirek.

"She looks kinda cool," Ethan said with increased interest. Mirek switched the mobile to Kat's pic and Ethan sat back, "stunning, but she'd eat me alive."

Mirek laughed. "She's mine."

* * *

Mirek collected Ethan, and they chatted in the car about their respective dates. "Remember, they're not bimbos. They're high-quality ladies out for an enjoyable meal with two respectable fellas."

The highly regarded restaurant Giangolini's came into view as the heavens opened. "You said you'd be paying," Ethan said as Mirek re-engaged drive mode to pull into the car park.

"Worry not. If you hit it off with Mia, you'll be tripping over me to settle up and impress the little lady."

"That's unlikely. If she's some basket case, I'll just leave."

"There's no pressure. Just relax and enjoy the night. Right then, time to make a dash for it." Mirek said. They ran under the canopy to limit their drenching and brushed off the excess rain with their hands before they made their way inside.

Mirek led the way to two women in the front lounge who'd stood to greet them. He introduced himself to the bronzed buxom beauty with flowing dark hair. He went to embrace her, but she retraced at his sodden touch, settling for a delicate kiss on her cheek. As usual, an instantly smitten Mirek totally forgot Ethan was behind him. Ethan glanced around them to see an equally nervous, fresh-faced brunette with a delicate frame under a leather jacket.

He put out a hand of friendship. "Mia?"

She nodded shyly. He held off his usual handshake, not wanting to crush her petal like hands. "Ethan. Pleased to meet you." They exchanged further pleasantries, and she giggled when he rolled his eyes at their friends, who seemed to have instantly hit it off and lost any sense of politeness.

The server bot arrived to take them to their table, leading them through the mahogany doors, which mimicked the doors to his house. It had been years since he'd graced Giangolini's. He'd been with Rachel on the anniversary of their first date. The food had been spectacular, but preoccupied with her work, Rachel had rattled on about a house sale she'd made rather than taking in the warm ambiance of the place.

As Ethan followed the girls and Mirek, Mia excitedly signalled to her friend when she spotted a celebrity she recognised. Ethan wasn't sure who they were, but they looked familiar, possibly a TV chef.

Ethan cringed with the thought Mia would only spout out girly chat and bore the pants off him. Mirek had assured him they were classy ladies. Hopefully, it wasn't just a setup for Mirek's benefit. It wouldn't have been the first time.

Ethan quickly changed his initial opinion as he took his seat opposite Mia. She was rather cute in a vulnerable way. Rather than engage in chat, Mirek and his date, Kat took their attention. They were sizing each other with how they handled each other's flirty chat. Having a ringside seat for the action was a delight Ethan had witnessed before. Mirek was certainly King of the chat.

Mia told Ethan about the coffee shop she ran with her mom, "Mom 'n' Mia's." Far from the young girly chat and sexually charged banter, Mia intrigued him with her passion for baking and how she'd styled the coffee shop.

Ethan shared his journey of how he'd progressed with the Tushi corporation and become a key management figure in the growing company. With the conversation slowing, Ethan teased some farcical tales of what happened at Tushi, but unlike the usual girls he and Mirek had dated, Mia asked more pointed questions to pick apart his tales. She was indeed a step above and destined for far more than running a little coffee shop, but she had a naivety that needed guiding. What was it with this girl? He needed to protect her.

He wanted to take her hands in his over the table like Mirek and Kat were doing, but to avoid any embarrassment if she retracted, he decided against it. Ethan was trying to keep the conversation light, but his head whirred about the possibilities of a relationship with her. He spurted out a question before he considered how it may sound. "Ever thought about, one day, settling down and having a baby?"

The shock on her face was not surprising. She leant back in her chair to take in his directness and consider her response. Ethan wanted the ground to swallow him up. When she returned, a flustered response about the coffee shop being her baby. She must have noticed the dejection on his face, because after her rebuttal, she softened the blow with a coy smile, "never say never though."

Was she just being polite? Ethan guessed she really wanted to shout out for the check. "I can't understand why anyone would want to deal with messy nappies," he said.

"Thanks for the image. I'll give the chocolate mousse a pass." Mia replied and burst into a fit of giggles, which broke the tension, and Ethan's sides also split.

Mirek and Kat looked at them in sync, which made them laugh even more. They were connecting with each other. Ethan put his hand forward to take Mia's hand, but pulled it back with the appearance of the waiter.

A pet hate of Ethan's was people who didn't know how to eat in a dignified manner. The last date who'd sat opposite him thought nothing of speaking with her mouth full. Mia, however, ate like royalty. Another tick of approval.

After they finished their meal and were finishing the wine, Mia seemed to become distant, hiding behind tiny sips of her wine, perhaps worried about where the date would go from there. Ethan was equally nervous. They'd got on okay, but compared to Mirek and Kat, they were like warring neighbours.

Kat jumped to her feet and dragged Mia with her to the bathroom. "Women they can never pee alone," Ethan said to Mirek with a comedic smirk.

"You'll be alone." Mirek rolled his eyes. "Kat's coming back to mine."

"Excellent." Ethan rubbed his hands together. Mirek had sorted the awkwardness to move things along just like he'd done at Uni.

"You're not coming." Ethan stared at his hands, but Mirek patted him on the shoulder, "take it nice and easy and you'll be okay with Mia."

Ethan had Chloe waiting for him at home, but there was something about Mia that had him intrigued. Chloe had showed she was more than capable of handling herself, but the more fragile Mia needed someone to care for her. He'd only just met her, but he wanted to protect her. If she wanted him to.

Mirek disturbed his thoughts. "In a world of your own? Let's wait for them in the front lounge."

After what seemed like an hour, Mia and Kat joined them. Mirek gave them some of his chat, before Kat gave Mia a quick hug and a peck on her cheek before taking Mirek's outstretched hand and heading for the door. "Cheers, Buddy, look after Mia." Mirek said as he opened the door for Kat. Mia stared through the window like a lamb being left by its mother as she watched them leave in Mirek's car.

Without Mirek by his side, Ethan's brave pretence also left. He remained seated on the leather sofa. He ordered men and women around all day, but outside of work, his words didn't flow. Mia had an enchanting beauty. She was smart and confident, yet vulnerable.

Mirek had urged Ethan to meet real women and find a deeper love than his Tushi. It all made perfect sense, but now he was wide open to more emotional pain. Mia was free to choose him or reject him. Was he the vulnerable one or the confident one?

Mia was still gazing out the window after the car had gone.

Ethan forced himself to ask, "where would you like to go next?"

Mia's head slowly turned back to Ethan and almost apologetically she said, "can you take me home?"

"Wherever my angel desires," Ethan said with renewed confidence as he raised from the sofa and like a true gentleman, he opened the door for her and popped his elbow out for her to slip her hand through. Ethan's tongue became free, and he talked all the way to her place about his memories from school. Mia seemed to enjoy listening to him and she told him how she'd missed out on usual schooling, because of her over-protective mother.

"This is me," Mia said, pointing to her oak door. Ethan thought her next words would have been to thank him for an enjoyable evening. He was gob smacked when she said, "would you like to come in for a coffee?"

"I would love to," he replied with a smile, as his body tingled with excitement.

Mia's brow creased. "I meant to drink coffee, not in for coffee."

* * *

It quashed any thoughts of sex when her house bot opened the door. As expected, her bot, Tyler stayed in the room like a chaperone. It was a little disconcerting knowing Tyler would both guard and learn, but it took the pressure off Ethan. Rather than making a move on Mia, he enjoyed a relaxing chat about the chilled-out music and his love of romantic comedies.

"Have you seen the wedding singer? It's over forty years old, but I still love it," Mia said.

"It's one of my favourites too. The old ones are the best."

"Couldn't agree more." Mia smiled, raised her glass, and took another delicate sip.

Ethan did likewise and took another gulp. Whether it was the wine or Mia's smile, he'd a warm feeling deep in his heart. With confidence the wine had given him, he gently stroked the back of Mia's hand. "I've really enjoyed tonight, but I should go soon. Work in the morning."

Mia politely replied she 'd enjoyed it too, as she slipped her hand from under his and traced her finger over the back of his hand. His body reacted like she'd stroked his crotch.

Ethan finished the last drop of wine in his glass, placing it back on the table. He took in Mia's brown eyes and thanked her again for an enjoyable night. He held her hand as she stood with him. Ethan leaned forward to kiss her, but she stepped back and placed her glass on the table. As her head came back up, he held her face in his hands and placed a delicate kiss on her lips.

She returned his kiss with increasing passion and thoughts of moving to the bedroom entered his mind, but in a split second her chaperone raised the lights, stopped the music, and politely announced his taxi had arrived.

"I'd like to see you again." He delivered a peck on her cheek and whispered, "to be continued or to be forgotten."

Mia returned his hug. "Definitely to be continued, but you'll have to be patient with me."

"No problem. We can take our time."

Although it was an abrupt end to their evening, Ethan had found someone to take care of his heart. He held in a beaming smile, looking forward to a glorious future with Mia.

The End

Ethan's story continues with "Finding Love in 2045," where we experience Mia's ups and down as she tries to find love in an ever more technological world.

* * *

Message from the Author

First, I want to say a huge thank you for choosing to read, "Time to Click." I hope you enjoyed reading Ethan's story, which leads to "Finding Love in 2045." The Awakenings Series concludes with "Awoken in 2046."

If you enjoyed it, I would be forever grateful if you'd write a review on Amazon and Goodreads. I'd love to hear what you think, and it can also help other readers discover one of my books for the first time. If you also recommended it to your family, friends and posted your review on your socials, it would be a massive help to spread the word about my stories.

If there was anything you didn't like or if you have questions about the characters, contact me on my socials and I'd love to discuss them.

Thank you so much for your support, I hugely appreciated it.

About the Author

You can connect with me on:

🌐 https://simonwardauthor.wordpress.com

🐦 https://twitter.com/s111ssw

📘 https://www.facebook.com/simonwardauthor

🔗 https://www.goodreads.com/author/show/21286594.Simon_
Ward

Also by Simon Ward

Romantic dramas with an eye on future technology...

Finding Love In 2045
A near future adult romantic drama.

Can Mia find love in a world where sexbots are the competition and instant gratification is the norm?

Her trusty house bot, Tyler provides the friendship to keep her company as she searches for the perfect partner.

As Mia finds her path to love. Will it be all she's hoped for? Or will she settle for what destiny brings her way?

Awoken in 2046
Mia's life with her dreamy droid, Tyler, is in full flow, but an unnerving incident at her friend's bachelorette party raises a fear that Tyler could do the same. She thought Tyler would always keep her safe, but now he could be her biggest threat.

Ethan (her ex) noticed the AI network expanding beyond his control, but when he raised his concern, he got frozen out of the corporation he helped to build.

Intent on protecting Mia, Ethan passes her a note at their friend's wedding. She tucked it away, thinking it was a message of love to win her back, but the message held a warning about a technological awakening on the rise.